Also by Micheal Maxwell

Cole Sage Mysteries
Diamonds and Cole
Cellar of Cole
Helix of Cole
Cole Dust
Cole Shoot
Cole Fire
Heart of Cole
Cole Mine
Soul of Cole
Cole Cuts

Adam Dupree Mysteries
Dupree's Rebirth
Dupree's Reward
Dupree's Resolve

Flynt and Steele Mysteries
(Written with Warren Keith)
Dead Beat
Dead Duck
Dead on Arrival

Copyright © 2020 by Micheal Maxwell

All rights reserved. No part of this book may be reproduced in any form or by any means, electronic or mechanical, including photocopying, recording, or by any information storage and retrieval system, without permission in writing from the publisher.

ISBN: 9798653196898

DUPREE'S REBIRTH

MICHEAL MAXWELL

Chapter 1

Dupree wished he were dead. Not literally, figuratively, no, literally. He hated the fact the sun came up on another day. He hated the fact that downstairs, maybe, were three people he despised. There were probably only two. His worthless son, Eric, usually slept until noon. Or so Dupree was told.

Today was a bit different than other days. Dupree reached over and turned the alarm off at four-forty-five, pulled the covers up tight around his neck and said, "Screw it." There are some reading this that will, using their best Dr. Phil armchair psychiatry, say Dupree was clinically depressed. Not so.

He was angry, resentful, frustrated, overworked, overpaid, under-sexed, under-appreciated, disgusted, and to sum it all up, he "had had enough." Granted, two hads in the same sentence might not be correct, but that is exactly how Dupree saw his life.

As he sat on the edge of the bed, he watched the digital numbers magically turn to nine-o-eight. He was three hours and eight minutes late for work. He didn't punch the clock or anything like that, but for twenty-five years he arrived promptly at six o'clock, one hour and thirty minutes before the first secretary. Two of the other men at the firm arrived at about the same time as Dupree. It wasn't written that they arrive at six, but it was followed as if it were chiseled in stone.

On the nightstand was a cell phone setting squarely on his iPad. He reached for the cell and using his index finger typed the words, "Not coming in. Sick." He hit send and laid it back down.

The bones in Dupree's knees popped, and the vertebrae in his lower back crackled as he stood. He groaned deeply and made his way to the bathroom. The dark yellow stream of urine struck him as odd. The last time it had been that color was when he stupidly agreed to a survival bonding weekend in Death Valley. Dehydration, they said. Stupid waste of time, Dupree thought.

The reflection in the mirror showed a face he almost didn't recognize. The dark circles under his eyes, combined with his sallow complexion, looked like the dying character in one of those Ebola movies his wife loved so much. He pulled off his pajama top and saw the thick growth of hair in the center of his chest that was nearly all white. The once toned gym-rat physique looked like the ten dollars per pound bacon his wife bought at Whole Foods. Soft, white, and totally lacking in tone, that was him. He shook his head.

Dupree sighed deeply and decided he would not shave today. He got in the shower and let the four, wall-mounted, massage jets and twelve-inch rain forest showerhead scald him. The water was burning his skin. It felt good. It hurt, but he was feeling something. He turned the thermostat down a few degrees. No sense getting blisters, he thought.

The water was like a healing balm. He closed his eyes as tight as he could. At first, he saw bursts of color, then those worm-like things his doctor called floaters, then black. Dupree let himself slip to the floor of the shower. The massage jets made a comforting rhythm on the shower's slate walls. The giant showerhead above him rained down as he lay perfectly still.

As he lay motionless, steam fogging the glass of the shower, he thought how much different his life turned out than what he planned. He was going to be an advocate for the poor and downtrodden. His law degree would be a license to fight the injustices of society, right the wrongs of racism, and be an instrument for good.

That lasted exactly ten months; his new wife got pregnant, his student loans were in arrears, and he was three months behind on his office rent. A fraternity brother was hired right out of school by a prestigious law firm downtown. He put in a word with the same alum that hired him. Dupree was in.

His friend was fired after the ravages of his cocaine habit proved too much for their heavy drinking boss. The alum died of a massive heart attack at his desk five years after Dupree was hired. Dupree was now a full partner and there was no one left from when he started, except a fossil of a secretary no one had the heart to fire.

The water was getting colder by the moment. Dupree stood to find the massage jets freezing cold.

He shut off the shower. He looked at the squeegee his wife insisted be used at the end of every shower and raised his middle finger to it. He was not going to do it. Not today, not tomorrow, never again.

The guilt he felt for not going to the office was weighing heavy on Dupree. His mini-revolution crumpled as he pulled open his underwear drawer. He dressed in his most comfortable Brooks Brother's suit and tassel loafers. He didn't button the top button on his shirt or put on a tie. He would do it in the firm's parking lot. No one would know.

For a brief moment, Dupree stood at the top of the stairs. From below him, in the kitchen, he could hear the screaming of his daughter's high-pitched nasal voice. When she paused for breath her mother took over. Their words were indecipherable, but the fight would break down to one of three categories; her lack of anything to wear, her curfew, or how unfair it was that all her friends were going to Cabo for spring break and she was not allowed to go.

As he entered the kitchen neither female looked his direction. His favorite cup was sitting next to the toaster. He poured his first cup of coffee of the day and walked to the sliding glass door overlooking the backyard. Alejandro the gardener was trimming the bushes against the back fence. Now, there's the life, Dupree thought.

"Would you please tell your daughter to watch her tone with me?" his wife demanded.

"Deanna, could you ease up a tad bit?" Dupree asked grudgingly.

"Arrgghhh! I hate that name. Why did you stick me with that stupid Disney princess duck around my neck! Call me Rene! I've told you a thousand times!" The girl did not ease up, she screamed louder.

Dupree glanced at the sliding glass door to see if it was going to shatter.

"See what she's like? I don't know how much more of this child I can take! What high school girl is allowed to stay out until two o'clock in the morning?"

"Ashley, Jen, and Heather, that's who! Would you please tell her she is stunting my social networking to the point I won't have any friends in a month!" Dupree's daughter commanded.

"Look, you two have got to stop arguing. Let's have a nice quiet discussion," Dupree said firmly but diplomatically.

"I'm not arguing!" his wife screamed. "There you go again, taking her side!"

"I'm not taking anybody's side. I simply would like a little civility."

"As usual you bend to the whip of the slave master!" Deanna threw her jellied toast across the room and ran out of the kitchen.

"Now see what you've done? Why can't you just once be a father and take control of your child?" Dupree's wife folded her arms across her chest and glared at him.

"Me? All I did was ask for a civil conversation. I can't communicate with someone who is screaming at the top of their lungs."

"You are gutless!"

Dupree turned back to the slider and under his breath said, "God, I hate that woman."

"Whaz up?"

The sound of Eric's voice shocked Dupree. He turned to see his twenty-three-year-old, standing shirtless, and in a pair of pajama bottoms barely being held up by his hip bones.

"Good morning sweetheart."

"What's to eat? I'm starved."

"You look it," Dupree mumbled.

"Whatever you want, angel." The boy's mother said with a syrupy smile.

"Hey Pops, you got any money?"

Dupree turned and faced the boy. He noticed a new tattoo adorning his son's boney ribcage. He was determined not to start a row.

"As a matter of fact, I don't. What happened to the forty bucks I gave you three days ago?"

"Oh, you know," the boy said.

"No, Eric, I don't think I do. Explain."

"Whatever," Eric grunted, opening the refrigerator.

Quickly scanning the shelves, Eric took the cap off a half-gallon milk jug and took three large glugs, and put it back in the fridge. Without a word he turned and left the room.

Dupree couldn't have counted to ten when the shrill cries of Deanna came from the top of the stairs. "Mom! Eric has been in my room again! He stole twenty dollars out of my purse!"

"Diane I am late for work. I can't deal with her right now."

"She's a lyin' ass bitch!" Eric roared.

"You can't just leave now! Why do I have to be the one?" Diane demanded.

"Because you chose to be a 'stay at home mom.' And you've done a fine job," Dupree sarcastically replied. Diane was still yelling and cursing him as the garage door slammed shut behind him.

The thought of running his car without opening the garage door passed through Dupree's mind. He hated the smell of exhaust. Diane would take Deanna to school soon; they would surely interrupt his attempt to suck up carbon monoxide. He started the car and sat for a long moment staring at the garage door opener clipped to his sun visor. Dupree sighed deeply and reached up to press the button.

The law offices of Atherton, Miller, and Chase were an eighteen-minute drive from Willow Creek, the gated community where Dupree lived. It was a fairly direct route. There was a left-hand turn when he left the gate, and a right onto Charles Street where his office was. Today, Dupree intentionally missed the green light onto Charles. The traffic was light and there was no one behind him. He sat through the light a second time. Then without signaling, Dupree slammed down the accelerator and made a hard, fast, left turn.

"Whoa!" Dupree's exclamation was a strange mix of glee and unsettling terror.

What had he done? He willfully turned the opposite direction of work. He felt an exhilaration that was at the same time liberating and totally foreign to him. Dupree laughed aloud.

"Whew!" It was as if Dupree was just saved from being hit by a bus. "OK, OK, now what?" His voice quaked a bit and held back tears. "I did it, I did it."

The dull murmurings of the talk news radio station that was the only thing ever played in his car was exchanged for the first FM station he came to that played Classic Rock. Some might say that Dupree was born again. That's not the case; he was simply freed of the shackles and chains that he dragged behind him like Marley's Ghost.

He chose not to kill himself. He chose to live a life free of despair and dread. The first chain broken was his job. He called in sick. Only three times in twenty-five years had he been sick enough to not report to work. What was he to do now?

The car rolled through the business district, never hitting a single red light. Dupree noticed small shops and little bistros he never knew existed. He saw a flower shop and a Chocolatier. Multi-colored flowers lined the street in hanging baskets. How beautiful, he thought.

When he finally hit a red light, he made a right-hand turn and another at the next street and drove the length of that street. He saw the names of law offices he dealt with on a weekly basis but never stopped to think about where they were. He saw an ice cream parlor and pulled over.

"I want an ice cream cone," he said to no one. Sadly for Dupree, the sign in the window read Open at Eleven. It was ten-fifteen.

"Oh well," he said, genuinely meaning it. He pulled away from the curb. It was okay. He wasn't angry. It didn't matter. He drove on.

He found himself humming along with the radio. As he drove, he realized he was smiling. Smiling from his heart. He meant it. There was no one to see but the stretching of his cheeks felt odd but nice.

"It's time for Beatle Lunch Pail, your daily lunchtime dose of the Fab Four," the radio announcer said cheerfully. Dupree looked at his watch. It was twelve o'clock.

Ahead he saw a sign that boasted The Best Burgers in Town. He looked for the drive-thru. There was none. He pulled in any way.

"Welcome to Billy's! Can I take your order?" A cute teenage girl smiled at Dupree as he approached the counter.

"Best burger in town, huh?" Dupree said with a broad smile. "I want one."

"Yes, sir. What would you like on it?"

"Whatever makes it the best."

"That would be everything," the girl said with a giggle.

"Then that's what I'll have. And French fries. I like French fries." Dupree felt like a little kid ordering for himself for the first time. It struck him he couldn't remember the last time he was in a burger joint. "And a coke. A big one."

"One Billy Buster, an order of fries, and a large Coke. Anything else?"

"Do you make chocolate shakes?"

"Best in town! I make them myself," the girl said proudly.

Dupree looked down at the girl's name tag. "Mindy. I bet you do. I'll have a chocolate shake instead of the Coke."

Mindy rang up his order, Dupree paid and she handed him a number. "It's kind of silly to give you a number. I'll bring it out to you."

"Great."

The small dining room was empty. Dupree picked a booth by the window. Before long, cars began to pull into the parking lot. Singles, couples, guys in work trucks, and four kids in a lowered Honda Civic all streamed in the door. Suddenly the little dining room was filled with laughter and conversation.

After a few minutes, Mindy brought a tray and set it in front of Dupree.

"There you go. I hope you like it. I made the shake extra thick."

This kid is actually happy to be at work, Dupree thought. She likes what she is doing. She's proud of it! The idea was so long dead in Dupree he chuckled. The first fry from the red, paper-lined, plastic basket burned his mouth, but the salt and crispy potato more than made up for it. The burger was gigantic. He tried to pick it up and realized he wasn't quite sure how to do it. He looked around sheepishly hoping nobody was watching. He chuckled at how out of practice he was.

For a second Dupree felt uneasy. He looked up and Mindy was watching him. He picked up the shake and took a sip. Without thinking about it, Dupree set the cup down, gave the girl two thumbs up and shouted, "Great!" across the room. Several of the patrons laughed good-naturedly.

The meal was a soothing balm to Dupree. He forgot just how good burgers and fries were. Diane was on a kale and arugula kick, and he recently claimed to have eaten at the office rather than face one of her Rotor Rooter salads.

As he tipped up the cup to get the very last drops of chocolate shake, he heard one of the guys at the table near him say, "OK, back to work we go!"

To Dupree's amazement, one of the others at the table said, "I can't wait to see how this job turns out."

These guys like their job too! It was the second time in less than an hour someone showed joy in their work.

As he stood, Dupree took another look around the room. These people are happy; he let the thought sink in. He reached in his pocket and took a twenty-dollar bill from his money clip. Mindy approached the table.

"All done?"

"Yes, it was delicious."

"Best burger in town?" Mindy grinned.

"Best burger and shake. Fries were pretty darn good, too." Dupree returned her smile and slipped the twenty under the French fry basket. "That's for you."

"I don't know what to say." Mindy's eyes welled up with tears.

"How about, 'Have a Nice Day!'" Dupree winked at her and headed for the door.

Back in his car, he realized he just spent forty minutes completely at ease. His stomach was glowing with the warmth of an old-fashioned lunch. There wasn't the typical knot he felt as he gobbled down whatever it was the secretaries ordered for the day. Some days he finished and didn't even remember what he ate. But this, this was comforting. Is that what they mean by comfort food? He smiled at the realization.

As Dupree started his car he came to a decision. Things must change. He must change. He would change. Pulling out of the Billy's Burgers lot he drove for the first time with purpose and a destination.

The guard smiled broadly as he opened the door to Citizens Commerce Bank.

"Good Morning sir," the guard said.

"Yes, it is." Dupree returned the guard's smile.

There were no customers at the teller windows. Dupree picked a pretty Hispanic woman in the center of the row of bored-looking tellers.

"May I help you?"

"Yes, I would like to make a withdrawal. Five thousand dollars from my account. 242-55-3820-01."

For more than fifteen years Dupree kept an account at this small locally owned bank. No one on earth knew of its existence. This was the first time since he opened the account he actually was making a transaction in person. Most of the time deposits were made by clients that he did little favors for, off the books, usually in cash and done by an associate or secretary, under the guise of 'loan repayment'.

The monies were anything but that. It wasn't illegal per se, more like things that fall into dark gray areas. The transactions were never recognized by either party. The receipts for the deposits were immediately destroyed by the client. The services Dupree rendered were arranging payoffs or indiscretions the client would rather just go away.

"I'll need my manager's approval on such a large cash withdrawal." The teller was polite but wasn't about to hand out five grand without someone knowing about it. "Just a second." She smiled reassuringly and hopped off her stool and walked toward an older woman sitting at a small desk just behind the row of clerks.

The woman scowled at Dupree and stood. The teller said something the woman frowned at. Without responding, she made her way to where Dupree stood.

"Good Morning sir. May I see some ID?" The woman looked at Dupree like she was about to catch him in a lie.

Dupree complied with a smile.

"You've had this account with us a very long time." The woman cleared her throat. "Funny we've never met." She smiled insincerely.

"I've been a busy guy."

"May I have your mother's maiden name, please?"

"Is there a problem?"

"No, no just making sure we are protecting your account."

"Do I look like a crook?" Dupree was finding his irritation beginning to grow. He hated dealing with this kind of self-important minor functionary. It was the reason since the first day he got his own secretary, he never went to a bank or paid a bill himself.

"Far from it." The woman said. "Her name?"

"Lugano. L-u-g-a-n-o."

"There is a lot of money in this account. We appreciate your trust in us. How is it that you chose our little bank?" The woman warmed to Dupree, seeing he was legitimate.

"A Swiss account was too inconvenient," Dupree responded without the slightest bit of irony. "Should I need to make further withdrawals, and not be able to make it in, what is the best way you can handle that for me?" He emphasized the word you.

"My name is Claudia Miller, here's my card. Call me directly and I can have funds wired to you." She slipped her card across the counter. She came prepared.

"And no fee of course."

"Normally there is a fifteen-dollar wire transfer fee. But, I think we can waive that for a good customer such as yourself."

"I knew you could."

"Alex will take care of you from here. Thanks for your understanding." Claudia Miller returned to her desk with a great deal of confidence in her ability to fulfill her duties as head clerk.

"Sorry about that," Alex offered.

"How old are you, Alex?"

"Twenty-five."

"You like it here?"

"It's OK. Not what I figured I would be doing when I graduated from college, though."

"What's your degree in?"

"Economics. Minor in International Trade."

"How did you end up here?"

"My mom is disabled and when my dad died, I was it."

Dupree reached in his pocket and took out his alligator card folder. He took the pen from in front of Alex and wrote on the back of one of his cards. He slipped the card folder back in his pocket.

"How are you with research?"

"I love it, why?" Alex gave Dupree a beautiful smile; she had a feeling she liked the direction this was all heading.

"One more question, if you don't mind."

"Not at all."

"How much do you make here?"

"Fifteen dollars an hour."

"I figured as much. I want you to go tell that old crow you're leaving. Then go straight away and give this to Paula Fiengale at my office. We need a new person to oversee research. Someone who understands modern methods and can find their way around the internet. Is that you?"

"Yes, sir. I am really good at digging up facts." Alex blinked several times as if to try to wake from a daydream.

"That's what I thought. You get a complete benefits package and insurance so your mom will be covered too. It is important you do it right now, do you understand?" Dupree handed the card to Alex. "I think you are just what we need."

"I don't know what to say." Her beautiful dark eyes welled with tears.

"Well, after you give me my money, a thousand in twenties and the rest large bills please, I think it is traditional to say, 'Have a nice day.'" Dupree smiled broadly. He was deeply touched by the loveliness of Alex's reaction. He thought for the briefest moment, if I were twenty years younger, I think I could fall in love with her. He smiled and almost felt like he was flushing at the thought, then immediately dismissed it as silly.

"Time for a change, old man," Dupree said, unlocking his car door.

The next stop required a bit of thought. Thomas J. Spalding, Clothiers outfitted Dupree from the skin out for more than twenty years. Diane bought all of the children's clothing. She had open accounts in all her favorite shops. Dupree realized he was clueless as to where they bought anything.

Spalding's would never do for what he needed. He picked up his phone from the seat next to him. He Googled until he found just what he was looking for. Five minutes later he parked in front of Buy Well Thrift Store.

Buy Well was located in an old supermarket building. Dupree was gleefully curious as he approached the front door. Like Alice stepping through the mirror, Dupree came through the doors to a world of wonder and surprise. Never in his life was he confronted with a store as he found in front of him. The place swarmed with people pushing shopping carts.

Men and women wandered the aisles with clothes draped across their arms.

To Dupree's surprise, the place was clean, well-lit and very organized. The clerks all wore royal blue vests with name tags. Dupree must have looked completely out of place, and totally lost.

"Hi, need some help?" asked a bone-thin woman of indeterminable age with a name tag that said, Ginger.

"This place is great!" Dupree exclaimed.

"We like to think so. Whatcha lookin' for?"

"Everything. I mean, a change of clothes. Can you help me?"

"Sure! That's why they pay me the big bucks!" Ginger gave Dupree a big smile. "Where do you want to start?" The woman was more than a little amused by this expensively dressed man.

"Well, jeans, a couple of shirts, tee-shirts maybe, shoes, socks." Dupree paused, uncomfortable with the next question. "Underwear?"

"Boxers or briefs?" Ginger asked, unfazed.

"Uh, briefs."

"' Bout a thirty-six? We just got in a bunch. Still sealed. Feel better?" Ginger laughed and briskly took off up the center aisle.

Within minutes, Dupree changed into a pair of Levi's. Faded, soft and oddly feeling like he had owned them for years. He picked out a tee-shirt that read, "Fire Fighters Do It With Hoses," and a slightly faded Harley Davidson tee from Tallahassee, Florida. True to his word, he took two packages of brand new briefs, three pairs of thick crew socks, and two button-up shirts, one dark blue, long sleeve flannel, one short sleeve, green plaid. He decided to wear the short sleeve.

Ginger showed Dupree the section of shoes that would fit him. To his delight, there was a pair of tan desert boots with crepe soles, just like he wore in college. Ginger checked the size and sure enough, his size!

"Well, what else ya need?" Ginger asked, surveying the fruits of her labor.

"Two things. A backpack or something to put this stuff in."

"Check."

"And do you take donations?" Dupree held out his Brooks Brothers suit and tassel loafers.

"Are you serious? Those are very expensive."

"Maybe somebody can get some use out of them."

Ginger cleared her throat and looked down at the floor. "My husband is going to preach at our church for the first time on Sunday. He feels the calling. Can I buy them from you? I mean, if you don't want too much."

"I believe I said 'donate,' that would indicate free. So how about I make them a gift to the new Reverend?" Dupree grinned at Ginger.

"Oh, God bless you real good, mister."

"I believe he has. I believe he has." Dupree said softly. "So, where do I pay for all this?"

"Backpack first."

The selection of backpacks was, to say the least, limited. My Little Pony and Frozen were out of the question. The zipper was not working well on a green canvas bag and another was scrawled with punk rock band names and anarchy symbols. At the bottom of the pile was a road-weary tan canvas pack with leather straps and a Yosemite National Park patch.

Dupree picked it up, shook it, and turned it over a couple of times. "Perfect!"

Ginger walked Dupree to one of the counters. "Lupe, take care of my friend here, would you please?" Ginger reached behind the counter and took out a large blue plastic bag. "This nice man gave me a suit for my Rich to wear on Sunday! Shoes too."

Lupe looked at Dupree and smiled. "Nice."

Lupe rang up Dupree's selections, and Ginger handed her the tags for what he was wearing out of the store. "Thirty-eight forty."

He paid in cash and waited for his change. "Let's put everything in here," Dupree said, indicating the pack.

Ginger stood hugging the blue bag with the suit and shoes as she watched Dupree.

Unnoticed by Ginger, Dupree took a hundred-dollar bill off his money clip while he was looking at the shirts. He slipped it into Ginger's vest pocket.

"For the offering plate." He said.

Ginger looked at him with a look of amazement, then stepped up and gave him a kiss on his cheek. "God's got something good for you. I just feel it."

"I hope so," Dupree said brightly. "I hope so."

Ginger turned and scurried up the main aisle to the back room. Lupe thanked Dupree as he left the store. His clothes and shoes were so comfortable he felt like kicking up his heels. But he didn't.

Dupree tossed the pack into the front seat beside him. He lifted the console and removed the envelope with the five thousand dollars from its hiding place and slipped it into the side pocket of the pack and buckled the leather straps over it.

It only took a few minutes for Dupree to get to the highway. He quickly looked from sign to sign. North ramp? South ramp? He found himself in a complete panic. Right or Left? Right or Left? At the last possible moment, he squealed into the left lane and on to the southbound ramp.

"Oh, man!" Dupree shouted.

His heart rate decreased as the car accelerated. Traffic was light as Dupree pulled onto the interstate. He used the control on the steering wheel to turn up the radio. Mile after mile he looked out the window, deep in thought and planning what he would do next. He put San Diego into the GPS.

Forty miles and thirty-four minutes later, he pulled off the freeway and into a rest stop. The huge trees and parklike setting were a surprise to Dupree. As far as he could remember he hadn't ever been to one. There were at least a dozen big rigs parked on the far side of the rest area. Dupree passed five randomly parked cars before he pulled into a spot on the far end of the lot.

This was just what he was looking for. He took the canvas pack from the passenger seat, tossed his keys onto the driver seat and manually locked the doors. As he crossed the sidewalk onto the grassy space on his way to the restroom, he was overcome with the urge to lay down on the grass. He argued in his self-talk for several seconds before throwing down his pack and laying on the grass and using his pack as a pillow.

The grass was freshly mown, cool, and a bit damp. Dupree spread his arms, palms down, and moved them slowly up and down. The cool sharp grass was a sensation he missed. As a child and even into his university years he loved to lay on the spring and summer lawn and read, or at night gaze at the stars. When had he stopped laying on the grass? he wondered.

He closed his eyes and let the cool breeze blow over him. He thought of his day. Dupree had given away a twelve-hundred-dollar suit. He smiled. He was wearing a time capsule version of his daily uniform from high school into his early twenties. He felt good. The biggest smile came though when he realized he had locked his keys in his car intentionally.

Somewhere in his thoughts of the beautiful Alex, the delicious hamburger and shake, Mindy's delightful smile, and Ginger's kiss, Dupree drifted to sleep. It was a slumber free of dreams, worry, or fitful, stressful, tossing and turning. He woke without any feeling of time passing. He looked around at the trees above, and the lazy clouds drifting overhead. I could get very used to this, he thought.

After a few more minutes of relaxing on the grass, Dupree got up and headed for the restrooms. After doing his business, he washed his face and hands in the cold water from the single faucet. The reflection staring back at him from the scratchy metal mirrors was smiling. The reflection was one he hadn't seen in a long, long while. He bent and splashed his face again.

Outside, Dupree studied a group of five men standing near a huge white truck. As he approached the group he realized there was concern they wouldn't be willing to meet the request he was frantically trying to formulate the words for.

"Gentlemen," Dupree greeted the group.

"Is he talking to us?" one man quipped.

The group chuckled, but no one else spoke as Dupree moved closer.

"I was wondering if I might be able to catch a ride with one of you for a ways."

"Nope." A gray-bearded man scowled and walked away.

"Sorry." Another shrugged.

"Against company policy," the youngest of the group offered.

"Where you headed?" A man in his late forties, with a three-day growth of whiskers, and the very short remains of a cigarette asked.

"North."

"Yeah, alright. Let's go." The man nodded at Dupree. "See you fellas down the road."

Chapter 2

Dupree and the trucker walked in silence until they reached the back of a grimy white trailer with Kamikaze Trucking in the upper right corner of the back doors.

"This is us."

To Dupree, the inside of the cab could have been a space ship. Apart from the steering wheel and gear shift, the gauges, dials, and assorted switches and knobs were completely foreign. Above the driver's sun visor were a variety of pictures, several of kids, cars, a woman standing on a rock, a big ugly dog, and a big-breasted, naked redhead on an ace of hearts playing card.

Between the seats was a homemade rack that contained a couple hundred CDs, none of which were in a case. A strange net covered in wooden beads the size of marbles covered the driver's seat. Behind the seats was a small cabin with a bed. The walls were covered in dozens of pictures similar to the ones above the visor.

"I'm Dupree. I really appreciate the ride."

"Larry," the trucker put out is hand to Dupree. "I can only get you as far as Bakersfield."

"That's fine."

"Where you headed?" Larry asked as they pulled onto the freeway.

"North. Not sure other than that."

"'Scuse me if it's none of my business, but you don't look like the usual hitchhiker. I don't mind givin' a fella a ride, but I'd prefer to know what I'm haulin', ya know."

"What gave me away?" asked Dupree, genuinely interested.

"The haircut. You look like a TV news anchor."

Dupree laughed. "Fair enough. I just parked my car in that rest stop. I am heading north, in hopes of finding some peace in this world. I'll just keep going until something strikes my fancy."

"Then what?" Larry asked.

"I don't know. Find a job, get a place and just regroup?"

"And what kind of work do you, did you, do?"

"Attorney. Twenty-five years." Dupree looked out the side window, then said, "Are you going to kick me out?"

"Oh, hell no! A lawyer that's seen the error of his ways? You got a ride with me 'til I get back to the barn."

Both men laughed good-heartedly. They rode in silence for the better part of an hour. Dupree napped his head against the window. Larry played music, whistled, and drove along in harmony with the road.

A series of bumps and the incline of The Grapevine woke Dupree. He rubbed his face with both hands and stretched his legs out in front of him.

"There's a lot of room in here. I would've never imagined," Dupree said.

"So, do Lawyers make as much money as they say?" Larry asked, not looking at Dupree.

"It really depends on the kind of law you practice, the reputation of the firm you work for, and the client you represent."

"Answered like a lawyer," Larry said sarcastically. "How about you?"

"Why do you ask?"

"I been wondering what kind of car you left back there."

"S550 Mercedes. It belongs to the firm, part of my salary," Dupree replied.

"What's a rig like that run?"

"The way it was set up about a hundred and five."

"Thousand?" Larry asked in disbelief.

"Yeah," Dupree said, almost embarrassed to admit it.

"I'm going to ask you again." Larry's tone was hard and his voice sharp. "Did you kill somebody, steal your boss's money, or something?"

"No, of course not. Why?"

"Well, who the hell would walk off from a car worth a hundred grand to hitch a ride in this turd hearse?"

"Me."

"Why exactly would a smart fella like you do that?"

"It was walk away or kill myself," Dupree said without the slightest hint of irony.

"I walked off from a bad marriage years ago. My wife got into meth." Larry tapped on the steering wheel nervously. "I'm not proud of it, but if I'd have stayed I'd been dead by now."

"How'd that work out?" Dupree was genuinely interested.

"Been married thirty-two years. It's been rocky along the way but we haven't killed each other yet!" Larry's tone changed to one of deep affection.

"What's your secret?"

"Well, for beginners my wife is a church-woman. That takes care of a lot of problems. No drinkin', drugs, runnin' around. I respect her and she respects me. Don't get me wrong, we been through some deep water."

"Like what, if you don't mind sharing?"

The trucker sensed that Dupree wasn't being nosy. He was looking for answers. Larry took a deep breath and looked over at Dupree. He saw the man sitting beside him looking at him like he was the Dali Lama.

"We tried real hard to have a baby for the first four or five years we were married. It just wasn't meant to be. So we adopted a baby boy, called him Aaron, after my wife's brother. Got him when he was six hours old. Right from the jump, I knew there was something not right about that kid.

"He was mean, even as a baby he would hit, scratch and bite his mother. She was patient and loved that boy with all her heart. She just would say, 'He's going through a phase.' I knew better.

"When he went to school he'd hit the other kids, girls included, he stole stuff and would tear up other kid's work and hide it in the trash can. My wife was forever going to the school. The older he got, the worse he got.

"Then when he was in the second grade we found out my wife was pregnant! Can you believe it? Guess that's what happens when you're not tryin'. The boy hit her in the belly one day, hard. It was all I could do to keep from killing him."

"Did you hit him?" Dupree's thinking kicked into defense lawyer mode.

"Not with my hand, my belt. Worked for me, that's what my dad did to all of us kids when we got out of line. He seemed to settle down a bit after that. I thought I showed him who was in charge.

"In '93 we had our little Sandy, our angel. She's my princess. I love that kid to death. She's twenty-three now. In '95 Andrew was born. Wait, I'm getting off track here," Larry smiled.

"Then, in eighth grade Aaron discovered weed. He started running with the school stoners. They were always getting into trouble for ditching school, vandalizing stuff. Then a couple of them broke into a house. They ransacked the place and stole a bunch of jewelry, small stuff, and a gun." Larry signaled and changed lanes. "Why do people insist on driving forty-five miles an hour on a freeway?"

Dupree looked down on the car as they passed it. "Age, I'd say. The driver looks ninety." They both chuckled. "Please go on with your story."

"Well, they got caught and wound up in the juvenile hall. Broke my wife's heart. But by then Andy was about four, and the sweetest kid you ever saw. Everything his big brother wasn't. My wife finally admitted that Aaron was just no good. When he got out of the hall I laid down the law and told him no more pot, no more bad behavior or next time he could rot in jail. That lasted about a month.

"That summer he ran off. Took six months, but he got arrested along with another kid for beating up a drunk outside a bar and stealing his car. The police called from Tehachapi. My wife was trying to make arrangements to bail him out! I took the phone and told the officer to keep him and lose our number. She was mad as hell. Didn't speak to me for nearly a week." Larry gave a sad little giggle.

"How long was he in for?"

"Three years. We didn't see him for quite a while, then he showed up with this Mexican girl. Wanted to borrow some money. Thank God my wife wasn't home. I told him he wasn't welcome around our place anymore. He called me every name in the book and even took a swing at me. I decked him, then kicked him until he scrambled back to his car, the girl screaming and cursing at me the whole way.

"Next thing we hear is he's shot and killed by a Hindu convenience store owner. Aaron was trying to rob the place, threatened the owner with a knife. The guy pulls a gun and blam-o."

"Sorry."

"Don't be. There was something in that kid's blood, genes or whatever you want to call it. I'm just glad it was him and not some innocent person he decided to steal from.

"So, Andy is in the Coast Guard now, stationed in Maine. Man, would I love to go back there. My Sandy is a missionary."

"A missionary? Like in darkest Africa, religious kind of thing?" Dupree never met anyone even close to being a missionary. Isn't that what they call the Mormon kids on bikes? That's America! You can't have missionaries to America, he thought.

"Kind of. She is part of a church group that is in Guatemala. They live in a small town where they work with orphans, widows and help the community with health issues. She's a nurse. They also have a group that does agricultural stuff, better growing methods, stuff like that."

"No religious stuff?" Dupree asked, not grasping the concept of what they did.

"Oh, sure. They have built a church, along with a clinic and daycare. They work during the day and have services and Bible studies at night."

"I've never heard of anything like that. We were church people growing up. My wife drags me to the church at Christmas in Artemus, she likes the seasonal music," Dupree offered.

"My people were all church folks. I've never been gung-ho like they are. But the older I get the more important it is becoming." Larry changed lanes. "So what about your kids?"

"A son twenty-three and a girl sixteen. I can't say I like either one. The boy is worthless. Won't, can't, doesn't work. Can't find, get, or keep a job depending on the season. The girl is a bigger bitch than her mother if that is humanly possible. Their mother has coddled and spoiled them to the point where they think they are entitled to the world and everything in it. If I try to correct, mold or punish their behavior I am belittled, berated, and badgered to the point I just give up." Dupree cleared his throat, "Too much information?"

"No, not a bit. I guess now I know why a guy with a Benz worth a hundred grand, and a hundred-dollar hair cut is ridin' in my truck."

An hour later the big truck took the exit into Bakersfield. Out the window, Dupree saw the flat, dusty, landscape of the great central valley. The area they drove through was mostly industrial, with a few car lots, garages, and run down, half-empty shopping centers.

"Well, my friend, this is where we part company," Larry said as he pulled over in front of an empty discount car parts store.

"Thank you for the ride. I hope you get to Maine to see your boy," Dupree said as he opened the door and tried to figure out how to get down from the truck. "Any ideas on how to get another ride out of here?"

"You seemed to do OK. Just be friendly and ask, I guess. Good luck."

Dupree landed a little harder than he hoped. He slammed the door on the big rig and stepped onto the sidewalk just as the truck pulled away. Across the street was a white truck that was colorfully painted with a tiger and the words Le Tigre Tacos.

Taco trucks were prevalent in L.A. but Dupree never frequented such lowly establishments. As he crossed the street he could hear music blasting from speakers on top of the truck. The accordions and the bouncy um-pa-pa beat were a pleasant change from the country music of Larry's truck. The side of the truck opposite the street was connected to an awning, and there were six picnic tables were several customers sat either eating or waiting.

Dupree found the idea of eating at a Roach Coach, as he heard them referred to, rather appealing. He took a seat at one of the tables facing the truck. The bill of fare was as foreign as his surroundings. Lingua, pastor, carne asada, pollo, what were these things? Burritos, tacos, and nachos he knew from Taco Bell commercials, but sopas, tortas, and gorditas were a mystery.

As he read and re-read the menu he became more and more uncomfortable. He could feel the eyes of the other patrons on him. He would ask the waiter when he arrived, Dupree thought. Minutes went by and no one approached. Then a man from the truck called out the window something he didn't understand, and a man from one of the other tables approached the window and was handed his food.

Dupree stood and cautiously approached the same window.

"You order here." A woman's voice came from a window to his left.

The woman was barely visible behind the screen on the small opening, and the poor lighting inside the truck only made it worse.

"What would you like?" she asked.

"I'm not quite sure. A burrito."

"Super?"

"Yes," Dupree replied, quite proud of his ability to order.

"What meat?"

Dupree panicked. He quickly looked around the wall of the truck for a list, something, anything that could help.

"Pollo, asada? Chili verde, Colorado?" the woman grilled.

Colorado, a word Dupree recognized. He wasn't sure what kind of meat it was but he assumed it must be beef because they have cowboys there.

"Colorado," Dupree said confidently, "and a Pepsi."

He paid and was rewarded with a robotic, "thank you."

Two cars pulled up and three men got out. A couple with two children got out of the other. It struck Dupree that not only were the people working in the truck Mexicans but so were all the people at the tables and standing in line to order.

The two kids quickly escaped their parents and ran and played around the end of the truck by their car. They laughed and squealed in some sort of tag-type game.

It wasn't long until a man called from the window, "Chili Colorado burrito, Pepsi!"

The man handed Dupree a large aluminum-foil-covered object and a can of Pepsi through the window.

"Thanks," Dupree offered.

The man in the truck didn't respond. Dupree returned to his table. This time he sat with his back to the truck. He peeled back half the foil before stopping to take a bite. His first bite consisted mainly of tortilla, onions, cilantro, tomatoes, and peppers. The blend was a shock to his pallet. He took another bite and reached the savory filling of beef, beans, and rice. Dupree was embarrassed when he realized he was grinning from ear to ear as he chewed.

The light was fading. The people, for the most part, got their order and left. Two men sat across from Dupree.

"Excuse me."

A man in a straw cowboy hat turned and gave Dupree an unfriendly look.

"Do you know of a motel or anywhere close I could get a room?"

"No." The man went back to his food.

"Thanks." Dupree regretted asking.

"Ask Chuy."

"Pardon?"

"Chuy. In the truck. He can hook you up with a place to sleep." The friend of the man in the cowboy hat indicated the man watching them from the small window in the side of the truck.

"Great, thanks."

"No problem."

Dupree stood and went back to the small window in the truck where he placed his order. He tossed his trash in the can next to the truck and took the last sip of Pepsi.

"The fellow there said you might be able to help me with a place to stay the night," Dupree spoke into the screen on the small window.

"Twenty." The man's accent was thick but clear.

"OK."

"Over there. I suggest the Caddie. Fits nice for a guy your size."

Turning, Dupree saw the line of four cars parked against the wall of the building next door. He noticed them before but figured they were abandoned or stored there.

"I'm not sure I understand."

"Those cars there? They are fixed to sleep in. They're clean and all. No bugs or nothin'."

"Mind if I have a look?" Dupree wasn't sure if he understood what he was being offered.

The man in the truck bent down, disappearing for a moment. "Here are the keys. You check it out. Then bring me twenty dollars and she's yours until morning." The screen opened and a hand with a large keychain came through the window. "Here take a look."

The keychain was a large plastic dog with a partial bone in its mouth. Half was missing, snapped off a long time ago.

"I'll check it out."

A car with its headlights already on pulled up next to the truck. A man in a bright red t-shirt and headscarf got out, looked around, and then approached the window.

The gold Cadillac Sedan Deville sat in the middle of the group of four cars against the wall. It was a late sixties, early seventies model. Dupree really couldn't tell. As he approached the car he could see the front and side windows were blacked out. Not with film, but with a thick coat of black paint. Unlocking the door, Dupree saw the lights of the dashboard and overhead come on.

The seats were removed and in their place was a mattress which extended into the trunk of the car. Chuy was right, the bed was made up with sheets and a dark green blanket. Dupree smiled and gave a soft chuckle.

"This will do just fine."

As he walked back to the taco truck, Dupree took a twenty-dollar bill from his pocket.

The man in red sat on the bench waiting for his order.

"Looks good."

Chuy came to the window. "House rules, no dope, no smoking, no whores. Got it?"

"No problem. It's been a long day, I just want some sleep." Dupree slipped the twenty across the small metal counter.

"I get here around six-thirty for breakfast. You can check out any time after that." Chuy took the money. "Try not to make a mess, huh?"

"No problem. One question. Is it safe? I mean after you close down."

"There will be two of my regulars on either side of you. They will take care of anybody who comes snooping around." Chuy laughed. "You're not scared of the dark, are you?"

"Nope, not scared of the dark. Just people who might try to join me uninvited."

"I got you. Won't be no problems."

"Thanks, see you in the morning. Say, do you know what time it is?" Dupree inquired.

"Almost eight."

Dupree threw his backpack into the car. He glanced around and noticed for the first time the car was up on cement blocks. No tires or wheels. It wasn't going anywhere soon. Behind the row of cars was a small battery charger and a small wire running to each of the four vehicles.

"Quite the operation," Dupree said as he climbed into the Cadillac motel.

Inside, the mattress was quite comfortable. The lights were controlled by a switch next to the door. To Dupree's amazement, the radio in the dashboard worked. He turned the dial until he found a soft rock station, adjusting the volume to a just-audible level.

Still concerned by the safety of his strange surroundings, Dupree put his backpack under the mattress and locked the doors. He stretched out, his head toward the dash and his feet in the trunk. He flipped the light switch and lay in the dark. As his eyes adjusted he could see pinpricks of light through the paint job on the window. A bit like stars, he thought as he closed his eyes.

Alone in the dark, warm, comfortable, and relaxed, Dupree took the time to think for the first time. It was eight o'clock. He wondered if anyone noticed he was gone. He worked long hours, so his wife wouldn't notice he wasn't around until morning. Neither of his kids would care, nor probably even notice he wasn't around until they needed money or his override on a decision their mother made.

His stomach gave a soft gurgle followed by a roll, and he let loose a huge comforting fart. Life was going to be good. The thoughts of the day, the ride, the abandonment of his car and his life, brought a big smile to Dupree, and as he drifted to sleep it remained on his lips.

A heavy metallic thud bolted Dupree from his sleep. He didn't move. He strained to hear what was happening just outside of his Caddie Sleeper. A thump, thump, thump on what must be the roof of the car next to him was followed by the same thud.

"Hey, you up?" A man's voice called out.

"Yeah, yeah."

"Well let's go. All the good jobs will be gone."

"Hold up, I gotta piss."

Light was streaming in from the cracks at the top of the windows. The inside of the Caddie was light enough for Dupree to realize it was daylight. He rolled over and tried to see outside from a small sliver of light in weather stripping of the window. It was indeed daylight. His shoes were somewhere in the trunk where he kicked them off. He struggled to position himself where he could find them and put them on before opening the door.

Backpack in hand, Dupree opened the door to the fierce rays of early morning. The taco truck was bustling with men buying breakfast. No one paid any attention to his exiting the Caddie. Wet stains against the building showed where the two voices he heard relieved their morning bladders. Dupree moved thirty feet down the wall and did the same.

The reality of being a hundred and fifty miles from home struck Dupree as harshly as the morning sun. His commitment to a new life seemed to falter slightly with the nasty taste of a morning without brushing his teeth. As he approached the window of the truck, Chuy saw him and gave him a jerk of his head in greeting.

"Breakfast?" Chuy asked.

"Not quite yet." Dupree slid the key to the Caddie across the counter. "Any coffee?"

"Got you."

Moments later a streaming styrofoam cup came across the counter. "Part of our Continental breakfast." Chuy laughed at his joke.

"Thanks. How far to hitch a ride north?"

"Mile that way," Chuy pointed at the highway. "You should get a ride there. You don't look like trouble. You ever done this before? Hitchhike, I mean?"

"No." Dupree took a sip of coffee. "Is it difficult?" Dupree sensed someone behind him and stepped aside.

Chuy took the man's order before answering. "Just stay off the highway. Don't get in if it don't feel right. A big guy like you should have no troubles. Good luck."

"Thanks, your Cadillac Inn was just the thing."

"Cincuenta y cinco" Chuy called out. Their conversation was over.

As he walked toward the highway, Dupree sipped his coffee and tried to plan for a day with no boundaries or expectations. He soon realized he controlled nothing. All up to chance rang with new meaning. He shook his head and walked on.

The Highway 99 North sign signaled his arrival. He positioned himself far enough away from the on-ramp to make it easy for someone to pull over. After nearly an hour no one did. The sun was high enough that Dupree guessed it must be close to eight o'clock. A guy in a pick-up slowed and took a good look at Dupree, then sped onto the highway.

It was a long while before another car approached. When it pulled over Dupree's heart raced. The blue Mazda rolled to a stop next to Dupree and rolled down the window.

"Where are you headed?"

"North."

"I figured that. I mean how far?" The young man driving the car seemed a bit unsure about giving a stranger a ride.

"Oregon or Washington."

"I can get you as far as Fresno. Hop in."

The door of the car opened to a world completely foreign to Dupree. The trucker the day before was a totally spontaneous act. This time it was part of a plan, a means of reaching his goal.

As Dupree settled into the seat, backpack between his feet, the car pulled back onto the road.

"I appreciate the ride."

"First time I ever gave a hitchhiker a lift. You looked like..."

"You're right, I've never done this either."

"I'm Artie." The young man smiled. He was dressed in jeans and a plaid button-down collar shirt. His hair was neatly trimmed and he was clean-shaven. "I'm going to a new job."

"First day?"

"Yeah. I am a Wine Chemist. New winery, new job, new life."

"Seems we're on similar journeys. I'm Dupree, and I'm looking for the same thing."

"You're a wine chemist?"

"No, no," Dupree chuckled. "I'm an attorney by training, but I've given that up in hopes of finding..." Dupree pursed his lips. "I don't know exactly, but it seems I am now actively pursuing it."

"That's funny. I was a history major when I went to Fresno State."

"How did you switch to wine chemistry?"

"There was this girl."

"Isn't there always?"

"No, not like that. This girl is just kind of the catalyst to the whole story. I was in this chem class, general ed. kind of thing. There was this girl who sat in front of me. She was really hot, so I decided to make a move on her. It seems that this other guy, Francis Petrocelli, I knew his name because of roll, my last name is Peters. Anyway, he had the same idea. One day we both moved to sit next to her, me on the right and Francis on the left. We started trying to chat her up, you know? She gets all huffy and snotty, and gets up and moves. She is such a bitch, that we start laughing. We got yelled at by the prof and almost kicked out."

"OK, then?" Dupree interjected.

"After class, we got to talking, and Frankie and I became friends. Frankie's family owns several hundred acres of grapes and a winery. His dad offered me a job for the summer, well, Frankie got him to offer me a job. Anyway, I really got interested in the whole wine-making process. Frankie's dad said I could have a job when I graduated if I got a degree having to do with Viticulture or Enological Sciences. So, I go for Wine Chemistry."

"That's great. So now you are on your way."

"The best part is, I am dating Frankie's sister. I really like her. I mean *really* like her. So, I lose a stuck-up girl, gain a best friend, and who knows? Maybe a wife!" Artie smiled broadly.

The pair rode along in silence for several miles. Dupree looked out the window at the dry, dusty landscape. The highway went from smooth and newly paved to the rugged texture of an Afghan airfield with potholes as big as a basketball.

"So I've been thinking. There is a truck stop called Klein's not too far from where I turn off. Might be a good place for you to catch your next ride. I mean lots of trucks and travelers."

"That sounds like a plan." Dupree nodded in appreciation. "So, what's the girl's name, the sister?"

"Angelina Maria Petrocelli. Old school, huh?"

"Wonderful! I bet she's beautiful."

"You know, not everybody would think so. But, she has a wonderful heart, and she always makes me smile."

"Sounds like love to me."

"You think? How do you know? I mean, how do you know when you are really in love, not just some crush?"

"I thought I loved the woman I married. The more I ride along this road and reflect on my life, I've realized I liked the idea of her. Tall, blond, great legs, could drink me under the table, my friends all thought she was amazing. So I married her. Two kids, later I realized I not only didn't like her, I didn't like being around her. My secretary was more fun to talk to. Don't get me wrong, I didn't mess around on my wife, ever. Not my style. But I know now I married a resume, not a person I loved." Dupree sighed. "Wow, where did that come from? What I'm saying is, it sounds like Angelina Maria Petrocelli is the kind of girl that a very happy life could be built around."

"I kind of think that too, but I'm a long way from marriage."

"So become best friends, buddies, lovers, be everything she wants. Make her happy. Then when the time comes, pop the question. I'll bet you anything, you'll know exactly when the time is right."

"You must have been a hell of a lawyer," Artie said with admiration.

"I had my moments." Dupree smiled and looked out the window.

Over the next fifty miles, Artie told Dupree about growing up in Bakersfield, his love of baseball, his older sister who died of spinal meningitis, and his passion for history. As the miles rolled by, Dupree slowly opened up to the stranger. He felt freedom in sharing intimate feelings, thoughts never spoken, and reactions to situations long buried.

Knowing he would soon leave the cocoon of the car's anonymity, Dupree spoke of his disappointments in life and failures, something he normally refused to admit even to himself.

"You know, this journey I'm on has opened my eyes to a lot of things I no longer considered possibilities in my life. The whole idea of finding a side of me is something I scoffed at in other people. When I was a kid we had an old LIFE magazine from the sixties with an article about people, adults, educated, established professionals who 'dropped out.' I remember as a kid thinking, why would they want to be hippies? They've got it made. They were well off, successful and had it made. I get it now.

"Sometimes the rat race gets to be too much. That's what happened to me I guess, I got sick and tired of my life. I actually thought of ending it."

"Why?" Artie interrupted.

"I suppose I was a coward. I couldn't face the reactions, the conflict, of telling everyone I know to go to hell." Dupree laughed at the thought. "So, you see, you can always make changes. You can always find a new road. I have! I just stuck out my thumb and a whole world of possibilities opened up for me."

"I'm glad you didn't kill yourself. Our talk today has given me some ideas and cleared my thinking on something I have been struggling with. So, you are needed in this world. Maybe just not where you were."

"That's very kind." Dupree looked at the young man for a long moment. "Say, isn't that the place you told me about?" Dupree pointed at a huge neon sign.

"That's the place!"

As the car moved onto the off-ramp, Dupree was hit with a feeling of sadness. He was enjoying Artie's company and the comfort of the ride. The task of finding another ride was again looming in front of him and he wasn't looking forward to starting again. But then again, he thought, this is the journey. Someone once said the journey is often better than the destination. So far so good.

The car came to a stop a few yards from the gas station.

"Here you go." Artie offered his hand to Dupree. "Enjoyed your company."

They shook hands and Dupree nodded. "If I knew where I'd be, I'd say send me an invitation to the wedding."

Artie laughed. Dupree opened the door and stepped out of the car. A strong wind blew across the parking lot. Dupree watched the car until it reached the road heading east.

"You sir, need a cup of coffee." Dupree's voice was blown away in the wind.

Chapter 3

The diner side of the building was noisy and crowded. An open archway provided an entrance to a misnamed mini-mart. The place was huge, with everything from nachos, hot dogs, and sodas to fishing gear and antifreeze. Dupree made his way past the CD rack, the free Cars-R-US newspaper, and the rack of lighters, knives, and 'legal high' synthetic marijuana. He chose a booth with the least amount of duct tape patches he could find and sat down.

The two-foot by two-foot Budweiser clock above the kitchen pass-through window was either wrong or it was a lot later than he imagined. Lunch was behind him and dinner was closing in.

"What can I getcha?" a very plain, obviously bored waitress asked. "Need a menu?"

"How about a hamburger and a diet soda."

"How 'bout it?" The waitress grinned. "Everything on it?"

"Yes, please."

"Comin' right up."

Resting his elbows on the table, Dupree slowly took in his surroundings. The crowd was not young, only one or two women in the place. Lots of ball caps, with every kind of message imaginable. Most of the tables and the entire counter were filled with men by themselves. Curiosity got the better of him and Dupree turned to read the sign above the cashier station: Occupancy 250. Dupree watched as the army of over-forty, pushing-fifty waitresses scurried from table to table, filling coffee cups, resting a hand on a weary shoulder, and passing a kind word or wisecrack.

Was this what they meant by the aging of America, he thought? Another ten years and the vast majority of the occupants in this room would either be deep into retirement or deep in the ground. How many of these guys ever hitchhiked? How many would pick up a hitchhiker? That was the more important question.

For the next few minutes, Dupree sat quietly, sipping on his water and returning the occasional nod from a passing trucker. He was at ease sitting in the booth alone. His thoughts were of his surroundings. The world he left behind was just that, far behind. What the next hour, the next day would bring was the source of curiosity. There wasn't a second of stress or worry, just an amused wonder about this journey he had begun.

"Here you are, Hon'." The waitress placed a large over-sized platter in front of Dupree.

"Thank you."

"Need anything else, just holler." Before Dupree could respond she was gone.

"My Coke?"

Another passing waitress said, "I'll get it."

The burger was passable, nothing like the one at Billy's yesterday, but the fries more than made up for it. Dupree couldn't remember how much money was in his pocket so he opened his backpack. It was between him and the wall. He unzipped the side pouch and took a twenty-dollar bill from the tightly wrapped stack from the bank.

The woman at the register was unsmiling, and she seemed bothered by Dupree's interruption of her rifling through the drawers below the register. He paid, then paused. The service was less than stellar. The burger was nothing special, the woman before him was just shy of rude. He decided no tip was in order and left the way he came, past the racks of impulse purchase junk.

Two young, curly-haired, bearded, college-age kids sat on the sidewalk in front of the restaurant. Their big green canvas backpack rested against the wall. Dupree couldn't imagine lifting, let alone carrying, the huge, metal-framed, combination sleeping bag-rucksack-duffel bag contraption.

"Give us a lift?" asked the blond one of the pair.

"Sorry, I'm on foot myself," Dupree replied.

"For real?" the darker young man asked in astonishment.

"Is that so strange?"

"Well, yeah. You just don't look much like a man of the road." The blond jumped to his feet. "I'm Curtis. This is my friend Mark."

Dupree offered his hand. "Nice to meet you guys. Where are you headed?"

"Yosemite. But we want to go in through Merced."

"Merced?" Dupree inquired.

"Obviously not from around here," Curtis said to Mark. They both laughed good-naturedly.

"It's about an hour or so from here. We want to camp on the Merced River," Mark explained.

"Can I ask you something?"

"Anything. But we don't sell drugs, steal stuff, or do sex for money," Mark said firmly.

"No, no, none of that," Dupree assured them. "You pegged me pretty well. Until yesterday, I never hitchhiked a day in my life. I was wondering if you could give me a few tips."

"Serious?"

"Never too old to learn, right?" Dupree felt like he was some strange life form completely foreign to the two travelers.

"Well, OK. Rule number one. Never tell them where you're going. Be as general as possible, that way if you get in with somebody you're not comfortable with, you can say, "Let me out at the next exit.""

"And for god's sake never smoke or drink anything they offer you. I had a guy give me piss in a beer bottle he pretended to open. Then he laughed until we nearly drove off the road," Curtis chimed in.

"Keep your stuff on your lap, no matter how uncomfortable it is. It's better than getting out and having them speed off before you get your pack out of the back," instructed Mark.

"Good one," Curtis agreed.

"Never take a ride from a female. They can start screaming rape, and not stop until you give them all your money, and pack, and stuff."

"And after all that you still hitchhike?" Dupree was overwhelmed by the horror stories.

"Oh, yeah, comes with the territory. For every asshole, there are a hundred nice people." Curtis grinned. "You never know until you go!"

Mark nodded enthusiastically.

"So, I want to head north."

"Good choice."

"Where would I best position myself to get a ride?" Dupree continued.

"If I were you I would get just between the gas station over there and the on-ramp. It's not highway and you're off private property."

"Little bit of a walk but will keep you from getting yelled at by the cops."

"Thanks for the help. I'll remember it." Dupree nodded and started to walk away.

"My turn."

Dupree turned. "What's that?"

"Why are you hitchhiking? You're not poor, or nuts, or a junkie. What's up?"

This new life was beginning to have a strange effect on Dupree. His inhibitions were falling like scales from a fish. He neither wanted nor kept secrets. The shielded, secretive, every word has meaning, and every meaning could be twisted life he lived for so many years seemed distant and lacking.

"I've decided to begin again. You guys are just starting out. You can explore the possibilities, your talents, the paths that fit you best. I am forty-eight years old. I found myself on the path to an early death, from life's pressures or by my own hand. I was doomed. The stretch of highway out there." Dupree pointed toward the highway overpass. "That road I understand leads from Mexico to Canada. Mexico was way too close so I headed north."

"When did you start?" Curtis asked.

"This is day two."

"You da man!" Mark exclaimed.

"So over there, huh?" Dupree said with a jerk of his head.

"That's where I'd start," Curtis replied.

"Take care," Mark said.

"Thanks, you too." Dupree turned and began the next leg of his journey.

Close to an hour passed, and the afternoon shadows were getting longer. Dupree lost count of the cars that passed him by. He tried different postures and attitudes with each new car that approached. Tall, strong, confident, tired, forlorn, pitiful, frisky, thumb held high, thumb up with a wave, and a dozen more attempts at being creative.

He tried to draw from his training in persuading juries to buy his case. Nothing seemed to work. Many drivers averted their eyes, some waved, several flipped him off, a couple of clever teen drivers pulled up and as Dupree approached they sped off. There seemed to be a strange curtain between the man on the side of the road, and the people encased in their protective cocoon of steel.

Of course, Dupree did make his own choices. One car contained a man so drunk he could barely get out a cohesive sentence. Dupree told him he was waiting for a friend. As the car jerked and weaved its way

DUPREE'S REBIRTH

up the ramp Dupree wished he still had his cell phone, but not for long. The peace of a life uninterrupted was starting to grow more cherished with each passing hour.

As Dupree began to tire of the rejection of his fellow man, his spirits were lifted by the sight of a slow-moving, mid-seventies Buick Le Sabre. The huge beast of a car seemed like a relic of a time long absent from the road Dupree found himself on. As the car drew closer and slowed even more, he could see it was perfectly preserved, gleaming gold, with wide whitewall tires and a vinyl roof.

The Buick pulled over just a few yards from where Dupree stood. He picked up his pack and dog-trotted up to the passenger side window. What he saw next gave cause for alarm and a sense of bewilderment.

"Hello." The voice was the strangest Dupree ever heard. "Can I give you a lift?"

Behind the wheel was a woman who was both elegant and grotesque, well-coiffed yet oddly disheveled.

"Well, where are you headed, daw'ling?" the woman drawled out.

"North," Dupree said, trying to decide if he was going to accept the offer.

"Well, today is your lucky day! I am headed for Modesto!" The voice was like Clint Eastwood pretending to be Betty Boop.

It was then that it hit Dupree. This woman was in fact, a man in drag. Not just a man, but a tall, raw-boned, big knuckled, sun-baked, western hero man.

The dress he wore was lime green, with sequins and thin overlays of sheer fabric. She wore large, green rhinestone earrings and a necklace to match. Dupree couldn't help himself; he looked down at her legs. Large, bony knees sat above thin, sinewy, muscular legs that ended in at least size eleven sandals of matching green sequins.

"Well, come on sweetie, I have got places to be and people to do!" The flirtatious remark was followed by a grotesque giggle.

Without hesitating any longer, Dupree swung open the heavy, Detroit steel door and jumped in. What could possibly happen in a moving car, he thought? The interior upholstery was smooth and cool. The window went up as soon as the door closed.

"I'm Christina." A large scarred hand with three huge gaudy rings shot out at Dupree.

"Dupree," he said, shaking the hand.

"Ooh, manly." The voice seemed less strained and an octave lower, more Bette Davis and less Minnie Mouse.

Dupree adjusted his pack on his lap, creating a heavy impenetrable shield for his crotch.

"So, handsome, where's your final destination?"

"Home," Dupree lied.

"Where's that?" Christina pressed.

"Vancouver."

"Canadian!"

"American. Vancouver, Washington."

"You're a long way from home! What do you do there?"

"Bookkeeper. What do you do in Modesto?" Dupree wanted to get the conversation off him.

"I'm a hostess in one of the top restaurants, Milano's. Have you heard of it? Oh, of course, you haven't. How silly." Christina giggled nervously.

The exaggerated feminine voice was beginning to grate on Dupree. He didn't respond, just chose to look straight forward.

"Did you want to grow up to be a bookkeeper?"

"No. I wanted to be a lawyer."

"I wanted to be a movie star. I almost was." The voice dropped again and it was overcome by melancholy.

"Really?" Dupree asked sensing a story coming on.

For the first time, he turned and took a good look at the driver. Christina wore a blond wig that was once certainly better styled than today. The large curls in spots didn't quite cover the netting of the wig. The hair was pulled down and forward, but still left the bottom of the thick, graying sideburns exposed. Below the sideburns, a two-day growth of beard protruded through the thick base of make-up. Dark pink lipstick covered a pair of thin, sunburned, peeling lips. Christina's neck was covered in whiskers longer than her face, like a man with poor or failing eyesight might miss. Dupree could see the skin below the make-up was covered with wrinkles. Some, like the one running from below her eyes to her mouth, was deep. Others around her mouth and eyes were shallower and many.

The most striking feature of the Christina mask was her eyes. The lids were covered in a deep emerald green eye shadow. A thick line of black eyeliner shot out the edge of the lid in a Nefertiti, cat-like, point that was matched by a similar line on the bottom eyelid. Crow's feet born of age and weather ran deep, and the eye Dupree could see was crossed by a deep scar.

When Christina turned to say something to Dupree he noticed a scar running across the bridge of her nose. The crowning feature of the make-up, though, was the buzzed eyebrows that were painted dark brown with an eyebrow pencil. Thick pencil lines went right through the short-trimmed brows.

"My daddy didn't want a movie star in the family. My momma was all for me being a star. She said that I was as cute as Annette Funicello. Do you remember Annette Funicello?"

"Of course," Dupree replied.

"I used to dance and sing with the Mickey Mouse Club. 'Beauty is as beauty does,' that's what wise men say." Christina's cutesy singing was bordered on sad. "Oh, do you remember this?" Christina paused for dramatic effect, then sang slowly and mournful, "Through the years we'll all be friends, wherever we may be. M-I-C-K-E-Y M-O-U-S-E." As she sang a series of tears ran down her cheek leaving a trail in the heavy make-up.

"A little before my time, I'm afraid," Dupree said softly.

"Oh, of course it is! You're just a baby."

"So did you get on the show?"

"My mommy saved and saved. She took in sewing, worked at the Five & Dime, and saved any way she could. She finally had enough for two bus tickets to Hollywood and three nights at a motel. We had appointments with three different talent agencies. It was so exciting."

"How old were you again?"

"Ten, I was kind of tall for my age. That seemed to work against me. I'm getting ahead of the story. Okay, when we arrived in Hollywood we went to Grauman's Chinese Theater and saw all the feet and hands in cement on Hollywood Boulevard. We saw the Brown Derby and all the places my mommy talked about for so long.

"We went to our first appointment and the man said something that made mommy mad and she started screaming at him and they threw us out. She was really mad for hours. She used to talk to herself when she got like that. Sometimes I would get confused and answer her, and then she would yell at me. She could be scary sometimes.

"Anyways, we went to the second interview and the man, Mr. Epstein, said he wanted to talk to me alone. Mommy wanted to stay and he said, 'Do you want a contract or not?' So she went outside to smoke. He was an icky man. He had me sit on the couch next to him. Then he touched me." Christina began to whisper, the ability to speak in falsetto disappeared. "He touched me you know where. He told me it was a secret and to call him Daddy. I didn't like him. His breath was stinky. Then he unzipped his pants and took out his, you know. He made me touch it. I didn't want to. He took my hand and made me." Christina's heavy black mascara was running down her cheeks. "Then he made me..."

"I think I understand." Dupree offered. "When did your mother come back?"

"She didn't. The lady outside Mr. Epstein's office made her wait. He did nasty things to me, ishy things that hurt my bottom. Then he suddenly stopped and turned me around and put his hands on my cheeks. I was so scared I couldn't cry. He said it was our secret, and if I told, he would come in my room in the night and poke my eyes out, and kill my mommy.

"He called mommy into his office and had her sign some papers. We stayed for a long time, like a month. I went to some auditions but I didn't want to sing anymore. Every time we went to the office he would tell mommy he was going to coach me, then he would, you know. I never got a job, so he yelled at mommy and told her I was a freak and that something was wrong with me. She threw an ashtray through his window. He grabbed her and started to push her out the door. I kicked him as hard as I could, you know, down there. He fell down on the couch and we ran away." Christina gave a giggle. "I liked kicking him."

"I bet you did." Dupree smiled. "So no more Hollywood?"

"No, we went home the next day. We still had some of the money Epstein gave us. Mommy took us to dinner at the Brown Derby. We saw Lana Turner, and William Holden, and a bunch of other movie stars.

"When we got home, daddy was gone. We never saw him again."

"That's rough," Dupree said.

"It all worked out." The feminine voice was nearly gone. "Mommy died when I was in high school. I moved across town to live with my grandma."

The two rode along without talking for quite a distance. Dupree saw a sign on the side of the road that announced they were entering Merced, Gateway to Yosemite.

"Merced," Dupree said, breaking the silence. "I met a couple of kids who were going to Merced. They were hitchhiking to Yosemite."

"A beautiful place. Have you ever been there?" Christina asked.

"No, I never have."

"Oh, you must go. The waterfalls are simply divine!" The falsetto was back.

"I'll have to do that someday."

"So, tell me about you, sweetie. All I've done is yack about myself. How rude. What is your life like? What do you do besides bookkeeping? Do you have kids?"

"Well," Dupree said, then paused, trying to decide what he wanted to tell. "I have two kids. A boy and a girl. The boy is in the Marine Corp, he is a medic. My princess is going to the University of Montana and wants to be a teacher. She wants to work with special needs children."

The lies flowed from Dupree like a bubbling mountain stream, without hesitation, conscience, or regret. He hated his kids. They never did anything to make him proud or happy. Even as small children they were brats, encouraged by their mother to scream and pout when they didn't get their way. Dupree tried to discipline them, punish them, and teach them to be responsible for their actions. His wife would come right behind him and pamper and undermine everything he tried to do.

The set of kids he was claiming was what he dreamed his children would be. This odd creature sitting next to him would never know the difference, and the thrill of bragging on this pair of idyllic offspring pleased Dupree.

"Oh, if I had children, I would want them to be just like yours. But, I can't have children. You know, because of what happened to me when I was little. Messed up the plumbing. But the Good Lord knows best in these things. I probably would have spoiled them rotten and they would have turned out to hate me. You are so lucky."

Suddenly Dupree felt ashamed. He wanted to cover his face, jump from the car. How could he have lied to this person who opened her soul and deepest hurts to him? The pain and shame that she lived with must be unbearable. He can't even tell the truth about his own children, rotten as they are.

"You know, Christina, I can't take any of the credit for the way my kids turned out. I worked so much that my wife made them what they are. She gets all the credit for the way they turned out."

"She must really be something," Christina chirped.

"She *really* is." Dupree felt a little better having told the truth, as buried in language as it was. But that was his stock and trade; twisting language to suit his purpose.

A few minutes later Christina pointed at a rest stop sign. "This little missy has to use the little girl's room. How 'bout you?"

"Might not hurt to stretch my legs a bit," Dupree responded.

They parked in front of the brown, concrete block building that housed the restrooms. Christina got out and went around to the back of the car. Dupree heard the click of the trunk unlocking but didn't turn to see what was happening.

As he watched Christina twist her hips and make her way up the sidewalk, Dupree realized how tall she was, well over six feet. Standing, her shape was totally masculine. Narrow hips and broad shoulders were a strange contrast to the elegant green dress she wore.

As she approached the restroom, her posture started to change. The head that was held so high and confident began to drop with every step. The broad shoulders that carried her forward with a sexy swagger were drooping and transformed into a defeated slump. Even her stride shortened and slowed to a hesitant shuffle.

Dupree took his pack from the car and went to the men's room. The trees in the grassy area blew and swayed in the warm wind. An elderly woman patiently waited for her dog to do its business in the Doggy

Potty Area. Dupree took a long, cool drink from the fountain and went back to the car.

    The car was warm so Dupree left the door open. He slumped down and closed his eyes for a minute. When he opened them again a tall man in jeans, boots, and a plaid, pearl button shirt was coming up the walk. He carried Christina's black gym bag.

    "Sorry I took so long," the man said in his husky voice.

    "No problem."

    The man started the car and said, "Next stop Modesto!"

    "How far is that?"

    "' Bout twelve miles give or take."

    The side of the man's face still resembled Christina, but the absence of make-up, false eyelashes, and lipstick so drastically changed the countenance next to him it was hard for Dupree to picture it as a woman again.

    As they rode along Dupree tried to process what just happened. Without a word of acknowledgment, or recognition, a transformation took place and left an odd space between two people who shared dark, disturbing memories. The bond of two strangers born of the baring of a troubled soul had a level of intimacy even close friends seldom share. What is it about total strangers that permits a person to open up their lives?

    There were events, memories, joys, sorrows, that even after nearly twenty-five years of marriage, Dupree never shared with his wife. There was no doubt that she kept secret people, places, and things he was never privy to.

Yet here sat a man, as a woman, who told of unspeakable violations of his body, ambitions, and dreams, to a hitchhiker within minutes of getting in his car. Would the story have been different with another hitchhiker? Did Dupree convey a trustworthiness that Christina felt comfortable with? Or was the pain and containment of her story so oppressive that it had to be released? Or, was it a tall tale like the one Dupree told?

Dupree wondered as he stared straight ahead, what kind of world he entered. He was a little over three hundred miles from home, yet his thoughts and contemplations were light-years from anything he exposed himself to at home. His world of clients, briefs, depositions, and shallow office interaction gave no space for quiet reflection. The idea that the people, who sat across his desk or who were seated at a conference table, held stories he never heard, stories in which he frankly held no interest. They were a means to an end, and the end was hours billed.

He thought of what being at home meant. A reheated plate from a dinner he missed half the time. A wife so enraptured with her important role on a dozen committees and charities, it was a one-sided conversation when they took time to actually sit across from each other and talk, and then it was just to have him put some event or other on his calendar.

Then there was the interaction with his children. Dupree wondered when they stopped greeting him at the front door with squeals of 'Daddy! Daddy!'

and became sullen occupants of his home that on occasion looked up from their iPhone or video game to acknowledge his presence.

What kind of father was he? How did things go so far off the rails? He realized, if he was as honest and open as Christina, he never wanted children. He married someone he really didn't love, and his job was the most important thing in his life. Or was it?

The nameless man sitting next to him turned on the radio to the same kind of music the trucker played. It filled the space now vacant of conversation. To his total bafflement, Dupree thought about his father.

"Your mother never remarried?" Dupree blurted out.

"Wow, where'd that come from?"

"I was just thinking about my family."

"Nope, never did."

"Did you ever hear from your father again?"

"We got a call from the woman he took up with after he left my Mom. She said he was dying, cancer or some other god awful thing. I was about eighteen I guess. She said he wanted to see me."

"What did you say?"

"I said, 'Hell no, why would I want to see that sumbitch now?' Then I hung up. She called right back but I told my grandma to just let it ring."

"Do you regret it?" Dupree asked.

"How do you mean?"

"I mean, do you ever wish you had gone to see him?"

"I never thought about it. So I guess not. How about you? What was your old man like?"

"My father was a very soft man. I don't mean in a caring way, he was almost obscenely clammy, soft white underbelly of a fish, moist, pale, I can't think of enough words to convey to you what he was like. His skin was moist, at least the part of it that was exposed. When he touched you it was like his hand was a thin bag of warm water.

"As a child, I remember seeing people shake hands at a wedding. I thought it was a cool thing to do, so I shook hands with several adults at the reception. The men, and even some of the women, shook my hand with a firm healthy grip. The men's hands were coarse, dry, warm, and even the women, although soft, were firm and dry.

"Then being proud of what I learned, I shook hands with my father. His hand was like it had no bones, it was wet to the point I wiped my hand on my pants after. That day I realized my father was not like other people. I think I was ten.

"I only saw my father once not wearing a dress shirt and tie. I opened the bathroom door not thinking anyone was in it. There he stood in his dress slacks and a sleeveless undershirt. It was as if I saw him naked. His skin was the color of milk. There was no muscle tone at all. His arms were thin and I could see veins clearly through his skin.

"My father managed a shoe store. He went to work there when he was in high school as a stock boy and never left. It was his kingdom. He worked six days a week. He got two weeks' vacation a year, and Christmas, New Year's, Thanksgiving and the Fourth of July off, if they didn't fall on a Sunday. The store was closed on Sunday. We were never allowed to visit inside the store.

"On Saturday, the busiest day of the week, we would sometimes meet him for lunch. We would stand at the front door at straight-up noon and wait until he noticed us. It was an unpleasant affair and I dreaded it even from a young age. He was so nervous about being out of the store, even though we were only three doors down at a small diner. He would constantly look toward the front windows as if expecting one of the clerks to come needing his help. They never came. He repeatedly looked at his watch, and would almost always take his chicken salad sandwich with him.

"In the fourth grade, as we were preparing to go on our weekly lunchtime with Daddy, I asked my mother if we could stay home. She pretended to act surprised I didn't want to go, but I knew she was relieved. He never mentioned our not coming. So we never did again.

"Years later I met one of his clerks. When he realized who I was, he began to tell me stories about my father. He was long dead by then, so the man supposed, I guess, there would be no harm. He was wrong.

"'Your dad was the biggest hypochondriac I ever met,' the clerk began. 'There were three of us that worked there. College kids, full of piss and vinegar. We would do anything to get him out of that store. One of the guys realized one day that he could suggest your dad didn't look good, and within the hour he would go homesick. So when he was particularly wound up about increasing sales or us not talking to a pretty customer, we would start in.

"'Are you OK?' one of us would begin.

"'Why do you ask?' was always his response.

"'I don't know, you just look a little pale.' The man laughed. 'Who the hell could tell? He was always white as a sheet. Why was that, you think?'

"'I don't know,' I replied.

"'Anyway, one by one we could comment on him not looking so good or was asking if he was alright, and sure enough he would start getting sick, and a few minutes later he'd say, "I think I need to go home. I'm not feeling well." Then we had the rest of the shift in peace. What a character. Nice guy, though.'

"I always knew there was something wrong with my father. He met my mother when he was in the hospital with meningitis. She felt sorry for him. They were the same age at the time, nineteen if I remember correctly. She was a nursing student. Her mother had recently died, and she and her father moved out west to be near her older brother.

"She didn't realize that he was naturally pale and pasty. She just thought he was slow to recover. Somehow, a fact I have never really understood, they got married. I was born a year later and my mother gave up nursing. I think she always resented him not letting her work, though she never said so. Even after I was in high school, she wouldn't even discuss it.

"I'll tell you another one. The clerk seemed to be getting a real kick out of talking about my father. Let him, I thought, he is paying for every second he's in that chair. We played another game with him. He was scared to death of leaving the front door of the store unlocked. I guess when he was starting out he did that once, and the manager found the door unlocked the next morning when he arrived. On the way to our cars, every night he would say, 'Did I lock the front door?' We had to park a good way off to leave the good spaces for customers. Just as we would get to our cars, one of us would ask, 'Did you lock the front door?' 'I don't remember.' And he would dogtrot all the way back to check. It always gave us a chuckle."

"I was never close to my father," said Dupree. "I hated that man. I intentionally made errors on his case and was delighted when the judge ruled against him. Immoral? Unethical? Undoubtedly. I really didn't care. He was a poor father.

"He died when I was twenty-eight. He retired, and not having his 'kingdom' to go to every day, he just sort of disappeared. I actually can't remember what he died of. I don't think I had spoken to him a year or two.

"My word, how did I get on to that?" Dupree hoped the man didn't catch his reference to being a lawyer.

Dupree was surprised at the journey he was returning from. He let go, opened up, whatever that soul-baring place was he wondered about. He could, and did, go there. It was easy.

"I asked about your family." The man shrugged.

"I guess I should have just said, I was an orphan or an only child."

"Would have been quicker. OK, we got six exits coming up. I am heading for the other side of town, to a wide spot in the road called Waterford. I guess the question is where do you want off?"

"I have no idea. I've never been here before."

"No reason to. Not much here but leftover Okies and Mexicans. We got a few Blacks. No matter. It's a good place to be from!" The man laughed at his joke. "I normally take the 9th Street exit. What's next for you?"

"What time is it?"

"Quarter to five," the driver said, looking at his watch.

"You got a couple more hours of light. You thinking about catching another ride?"

"How far is Sacramento from here?" Dupree queried.

"Couple of hours."

"I don't think I would want to chance hitchhiking after dark."

"There are a couple of cheap motels, a breakfast house, at the exit I'm taking. You'd be set for the night."

"That sounds like a smart option." Dupree agreed.

The traffic was heavy coming off the freeway. As the car pulled up in front of a motel, the driver smiled at Dupree and said, "Here you go, partner. I hope you get home safe and sound."

"I really appreciate the ride and conversation." Dupree opened the door and grabbed his bag.

The door closed with a solid thud. Behind him, Dupree heard the window go down and a familiar voice, "Oh, sweetie, you forgot something!" Christina called out.

Dupree turned to see the man sliding across the seat, his arm outstretched and his fist closed.

"What's that?" Dupree responded.

"Here!"

As Dupree moved back to the car, the fist bobbed slightly. He reached toward the fist and the man dropped several folded bills in Dupree's hand.

"Oh, no, you don't need to..."

"Too late," Christina squealed and the car sped away from the curb, and pulled a U-turn. A big hand shot above the roof of the car and waved good-bye.

Dupree was holding seventeen dollars.

Chapter 4

The motel was clean, and the bed was a relief to Dupree's tired body. He was so tired he barely noticed the heavy footsteps outside his room. The drivers of the two dozen work trucks and eighteen-wheelers parked around the motel lot came and went all night. Dupree heard the first three or four, but after a long hot shower, nothing was going to disrupt his sleep.

Around nine o'clock the next morning Dupree checked out of the motel and was faced with choosing between Smitty's Diner and Los Gatos Café. It was way too early for Mexican and the parking lot was full around Smitty's. It seemed the best option.

Dupree tossed his pack into the booth and slid in behind it. A woman in her late fifties welcomed him and gave him a menu. The table was a bit sticky, so when a young Mexican man brought him water and silverware, Dupree wiped the table with a napkin dipped in his water.

The restaurant was almost empty except for a few tables with senior citizens, alone and with partners. Where were the people all the cars belonged to? It seemed like the place was sealed in a time capsule. Everything about it screamed the 1970s. It was just like him. He was like a person who had been locked up for twenty years. His work so engulfed him, his life was protected by a cocoon of receptionists, secretaries, long hours, and a protective wall between him and the rank and file man on the street.

His vacations, both of them in twenty years, were spent in Europe. His wife and kids made the annual pilgrimage to her parents in upstate New York, a summer visit to Disney World, and a Christmas shopping trip to New York City. Dupree was grateful he was not included. Actually, as he thought about it, he wasn't even invited. He chuckled at the thought.

Business trips were airport to hotel, to dinner, to meeting, to hotel, to meeting, to the airport and home. It could have been Washington D.C., Las Vegas, Chicago, Pittsburgh, or Corn County Kansas, he couldn't tell one from the other. He was driven, focused, and productive. That's what mattered, that's what made money, and got him a partnership, or at least it did. It was also what got him here.

It was his second night on the road. He could have continued on last night, but truth be told, he was afraid. This was his third day. Dupree pondered if he should be farther along. What for? he thought, I'm not going anywhere.

"Decide what you're having?" the waitress asked, returning to the table.

"I would suppose the wise thing to do since the menu claims World Famous Pancakes would be to have pancakes. How do they come?"

"Fried mostly." The waitress waited for a laugh. Dupree obliged with a courtesy chuckle.

"Then I will have some fried pancakes. Do you have bacon? I would like bacon."

"Any eggs?"

"No, I think pancakes and lots of bacon sound just like what I need. And coffee." Dupree gave the waitress a big smile. It felt good. He didn't smile much. His doctor certainly wouldn't smile at his order, and that brought a smile to his face as well.

"Back in a jiff." The waitress turned and nearly ran into a boy of about six or seven who was racing to a booth.

"Marcus! Watch where you're going! Say excuse me!" Dupree turned to see an attractive woman of about thirty, with a tight grasp on a pre-school little girl. "So sorry, ma'am."

"He's fine, just excited to get some pancakes. I know the type. I got seven grandkids, all boys!"

The woman slid into the booth. The young boy was already in position with his back to Dupree. The waitress appeared with a high chair and put it at the end of the table. The woman gave Dupree an embarrassed but lovely smile. He nodded and returned her smile.

"Can I get the big stack and two extra plates? And two small glasses of milk."

"I want lots of milk!" the little boy insisted.

"We'll see," his mother said, trying to calm the excited boy.

"We have a free children's plate for the little one here if you'd like."

"Oh, that would be wonderful, thank you. You hear that Merci, your own special plate."

"I'll get you a big boy glass of milk and if you want one, I'll get you a refill." The waitress winked at the mother.

"Back in a flash."

The woman spoke quietly and kindly to her son. Within moments he calmed down and was chatting with his mother.

"Here you are sweetie, you gonna need anything else?"

"No, this looks delicious, thank you." The woman smiled up at the waitress. She was very pretty.

Dupree looked down at the plate in front of him. Again he was struck by how something so simple could be so wonderful. He spent years eating granola and horrible smoothie concoctions his wife whipped up when what he really wanted was the kind of breakfast his mom made when he was a kid.

The sight of pancakes and bacon reminded him of his mother. Funny, he thought, when was the last time I thought of her? Dupree's mother died a couple of years after he got married. She died probably at a time he needed her most. She always understood him. He distanced himself from her around his junior year of high school. He was terribly embarrassed by his father, and unfortunately, they never went anywhere without each other. Oddly, he was now struck with what a wonderful thing that was. He hadn't gone anywhere with his wife in years, other than the obligatory commitments that his work and her social nonsense required.

Dupree tried to bring up an image of his mother in his mind. Over and over he tried to find the pretty, auburn-haired woman he loved so much. Instead, he repeatedly saw the bone-thin, skeletal shell of her lying in a hospital bed being eaten alive by cancer. He only saw her once after she became ill. A call from his uncle warned he should come quickly if he wanted to see her before she died. It couldn't have come at a worse time; he was a new hire at the firm and was preparing his first big case.

Dupree recalled the look his senior partner gave him when he asked if he should take time to see his mother. The handsomely dressed, manicured, graying man, with the permanent tan and perfect hair looked at him like he was insane.

"I don't have to if you think..."

"You say she's dying?" his boss interrupted.

"Yes, sir."

"Do you have another mother?"

"No, sir?"

"We are attorneys at law. It is our chosen profession. However, we are sons, husbands, and fathers, first and foremost. Don't make me question my decision to bring you into our family. Leave, go, get out." The quintessential lawyer rose for his closing remark. "Give my condolences to your family and kiss your mother, God bless her, for me."

Though it was years ago, Dupree burned with shame. He should have taken that admonition to heart. If truth be told, by the time he returned from his mother's funeral it was all but forgotten.

The image of his mother's closed coffin, with a picture sitting atop it from some long-ago photographer's studio, came clearly to his mind. She was quite lovely.

His mother always wore dresses. Dupree never saw her in pants, a skirt, shorts or anything other than a dress. In the heat of summer they may have been sleeveless, in winter a heavier material but, rain or shine, she was in a dress, usually of her own making, from morning to evening. She was always up and dressed when he came out of his room. As he aged and stayed up later than his parents, he never saw her in a robe or any kind of sleepwear.

His parents were such an odd match. Dupree even at a very young age wondered how his beautiful mother could be married to the thick droopy lipped, homely man that was his father. Even apart from the appearance, their temperaments were so very different. Where his father lacked confidence, his mother was always self-assured. She could grow impatient with a salesman, a neighbor with a yapping dog, or Dupree's childhood mischief. His father would almost cower at the thought of confronting or complaining about anything.

There was a time around the fourth grade when Dupree fantasized elaborate plans for stealing his mother away, marrying her, and living happily ever after in a cabin in the woods. In college, Dupree recalled his Oedipal imaginings, and realized they fell short of classic because he didn't dream of killing his father or having him die. In his psychology class, Dupree remembered thinking, if the professor had only met his father he would understand why it would have been like killing some poor defenseless animal.

He thought of the times when they would work on a puzzle at the kitchen table, while his father would sleep slouching in a chair in the living room.

"He works so hard," she would always say.

Those were his best memories of his childhood; hot cocoa and long talks about school and his day. She would tell of growing up in Virginia.

His mother's maternal Grandfather Warren was a five-term member of the Commonwealth of Virginia's House of Delegates. Warren's wife Louisa was from a rich multi-generational plantation family, who proudly spoke of their direct lineage to Thomas Jefferson's father Peter.

Dupree's grandmother, Faith, was raised in a wealthy, aristocratic home. She spent her youth going to exclusive summer camps, private schools, coming out parties, and debutante balls. The photos in his mother's family albums looked like scenes from Gone with the Wind. Their lives were charmed, pampered, and part of a world Dupree's mother never knew.

At eighteen Faith went to the College of William and Mary, the second oldest university in America. It boasts itself as to where a young George Washington got his surveyors license. Her family's name was on several buildings and statues. As the daughter of one of the founding families, she was treated like a princess. She was pledged to the most prestigious sorority and roomed in the building that once housed the President of the College. There were twelve bedrooms, and each was assigned to a young lady of an equally impressive pedigree.

Dupree's mother loved to tell the story of one warm spring day when Faith saw a young man, with curly hair and a crisp white shirt, sitting under an elm reading a book. She thought he was so handsome she pretended to stumble and dropped her books at his feet. His mother told the story often as the time approached for Dupree to leave for college. "Always be open to possibilities!" she would smile and say.

The handsome young man was Dupree's grandfather, Calvin. In the fairytale way his mother told the story, he was noble of heart, handsome of face, and without a cent. He won a scholarship and planned to study engineering. Over the course of the next four years, they fell deeply in love, much to the dismay of Faith's parents.

They courted in a sweet, old-fashioned way. Faith's young man, as she called him, would bring flowers he clipped from one of the gardens on campus. They would take long walks in the moonlight and Calvin would sing a popular song of the day. They wrote long letters of their dreams and aspirations: hers of family, children and growing old together; his of their travels, great adventures, building roads and bridges in exotic locales and loving her until he died.

Her family wasn't pleased with his background, but his education and plans for a career in engineering made his parent's lack of social status more palatable. Everything was bright in their future until the night of the Grand Spring Cotillion. When, just before leaving to collect Faith, Calvin received a telegram reporting his father had fallen ill and he must come home.

It turned out that 'just fallen' was an exaggeration. He was diagnosed with prostate cancer months before but didn't want to worry his son. He was so proud to have a son about to graduate college. Now in the final stages of the disease, he would not live to see Calvin arrive.

Calvin's family owned a small grocery store. His father was the butcher, his mother worked the counter. It was the family's income, their anchor in hard times. It was their church and social club. It wasn't just a business, it was their world. During World War II the store helped collect scrap.

The dreams of travel and building wondrous things seemed to be lowered into the ground with his father's coffin. Dozens of friends, customers, and family members gathered on the bright, beautiful spring day to pay their respects, but Calvin's world couldn't be darker.

Calvin didn't return to school, he didn't build anything other than shelves in the store for the next twenty years. To the dismay of her parents, Faith married Calvin. She got her dream of marriage and children; the only dream that didn't come true was growing old together.

From a young age, Dupree's mother and her brother stocked the shelves, swept up, and took out the trash, until he got drafted. She worked in the store after school and in the summer when she wasn't at camp, a tradition her mother refused to let go of. Her grandparents secretly paid for it. The only lie Faith ever told Calvin was that she saved the money every year. When Faith died of breast cancer, Calvin couldn't stand to look toward the register and not see her. He sold the store and they moved to California where her brother got a job in the aerospace industry after leaving the army.

Dupree's mother finished high school and enrolled in nursing school shortly after. She loved her studies and she seemed to be born to care for the sick. Her nurse's uniform was always the whitest and crispest of any girl in her class.

It was nursing that brought her together with his father. Dupree wished she'd become a teacher.

"More coffee?" The waitress's words brought Dupree back from his thoughts.

"That would be wonderful," he replied.

As he placed two strips of bacon in a pancake and rolled it up, the woman's phone in the next booth rang.

"No, I'm still stuck in Modesto." She frowned as she spoke. "Three hundred. No, they declined my card. Where would I find a Western Union? I'm in some edge of the highway diner. This neighborhood is really scuzzy." She paused and took a sip of water. When she looked up, Dupree saw tears streaming down her face. "No, I know you can't. I'll figure something out. I have no idea where a Bank, or Western Union, or anything is. I'm scared to death of what a taxi would cost. It would wipe me out. Huh-uh, I've got enough for food for the kids and the motel for another night. I know Gran. It's Okay. I love you too. Yes, as soon as I know."

She looked up and caught Dupree watching her. "Sorry."

"No, excuse me. I didn't mean to eavesdrop. What's happened?"

"My transmission. It's in the shop up the street. They charged three hundred dollars to fix it. For some reason, my credit card was declined." She teared up again. "The creepy guy at the shop offered to make me a trade if you know what I mean." She looked at her children.

"Seriously?" Dupree was stunned. "Did you call the police?"

"He said, she said.' Right?" She looked down at her plate. The conversation was over for the moment.

Once again the personal space between strangers lifted like a curtain. Dupree pondered how he could help. There was more than enough money in his pack. He could pay for the repair and not feel it. But under what guise could a strange man in a greasy coffee shop offer help?

"Where is home?"

"Down by San Diego, but this is as far as we made it." The woman smiled and shrugged.

"I see. Where were you going?" Dupree tried to sound friendly and concerned.

"Nampa, Idaho. My family is there."

"Quite a fix you're in. Maybe we can help each other."

"No thank you," she said firmly.

"Hear me out," Dupree answered. "I need to get to Washington, I don't have a car. I do have some money. Enough to pay for the repairs. I could help drive."

"That's very kind, but..."

"What's your other option?"

"I could walk to the Western Union. I Googled it. It's an hour and fifteen-minute walk."

"They're going to love that." Dupree smiled and nodded toward the children. "Think about it. It would be worth it to me to not have to hitchhike anymore."

"Thank you but..."

"Where is your car?" Dupree pressed.

"Jerry's Transmission, just up the street."

"When I finish, I'll go talk to him."

"And say what?"

"What was it the guy in the movie said? I'll make him an offer he can't refuse." Dupree smiled reassuringly. "At least let me do that for you."

"Well, I..."

"I insist."

"Okay." The woman looked at Dupree for a long moment. "I'm Krista Engels."

"I'm Dupree. It's going to be fine."

"Who did you speak to at the repair shop?"

"Jerry, the owner."

"Alright, let me see what I can do." Dupree picked up the last piece of bacon and stood up. "Sit tight, I'll be right back."

On the way to the door Dupree stopped at the register and paid for his breakfast, and Krista and her kids. The waitress got a healthy tip, too.

Out on the street, the sun was glaring down from a clear azure sky. Dupree looked down both sides of the street. Krista was right, this neighborhood was nasty. Off to the left Dupree spotted Jerry's. The sign was blue and the lettering was peeling away.

Lots of people were roaming both sides of the street. As he passed the first man, the stench fouled the late morning air. As he looked closer, the man leaning against the wall of an abandoned building was passed out. His grey work pants were stained down the inside seam of both legs where he soiled himself. Dupree winced and walked a little quicker.

A man with long tangled hair sat in the doorway of the next building. He wore a filthy white ball cap that read '99% Unicorn.' His beard was grossly uneven and down to his chest. It was clear he couldn't focus, and his eyes drooped and his head nodded as Dupree passed.

Several people shuffled and stumbled past Dupree as he made his way along the street. Coming toward him was a figure pulling a makeshift cart. As he approached, Dupree could see he was wrapped head to toe in black garbage bags, round and round and held tight with silver duct tape, like a twenty-first-century mummy. His huge gray beard, nose, eyes, and forehead were the only part of his humanity that was exposed. The cart was loaded with bundles of black garbage bags and rolled unevenly on bent bicycle wheels.

"What are you lookin' at?" the man growled as Dupree moved to one side letting him and the cart pass.

"What kind of hell is this place?" Dupree mumbled to himself as he continued up the street.

There was an empty lot next to the transmission shop. Just on the edge a man with a cart similar to Tape Man, and a woman with a huge clear plastic bag of water bottles slung over her shoulder, were talking as Dupree approached.

"Where were you?" the man asked her.

"Just up there. They took my cart and my recycles," the woman shot back.

"Who did, Dude?"

"I don't know. I was takin' a sip with some of the guys."

"They took everything?"

The woman was dark, Mexican probably, dressed in a pair of tight jeans and a western-style shirt. A large roll of fat extended over the top of the jeans, nearly covering her large belt buckle. "This is what I got left!"

"Let's go find 'em. I'll help. Nobody can be stealin' from you. Not when I'm around." The man didn't look right or left and took off across the street pulling his cart. Cars honked and swerved to miss the man and cart. The woman trotted along behind but was much more mindful of the traffic.

Jerry's Transmission Repair was, in a word, filthy. It was as if it were repeatedly sprayed with grease, layer upon layer covering years of dust and dirt. The floors were black, the walls showed running oily trails, and the work area was a gooey collection of greasy tools.

Dupree stood at the open roll-up door and waited for signs of movement. He was hesitant to walk on the greasy floor of the shop and positioned himself just short of the mess. After several minutes passed, Dupree was growing impatient. He cleared his throat with a blustery attempt to be noticed. Finally, he couldn't stand the wait any longer.

"Hello, is anyone home?" After a few moments, he tried again. "Hey! Anybody here?"

From a side door near the back of the shop, a shadow of a man entered the shop. "I'm here! Whatcha need?" the voice called out.

"I need to discuss a job you did," Dupree replied, louder than he intended.

"Thirty days or three thousand miles. Got a receipt?" The man belonging to the voice came out from the shadows.

Jerry was about forty. Like his shop, he was greasy head to foot. The color of the blue overalls he wore was only detectable in the creases and around the collar. The t-shirt under the jumpsuit looked like it was as permanent as his skin. He was unshaven and his hair was slicked back, in desperate need of washing.

As Jerry approached the front of the shop, Dupree reached in his hip pocket and got his wallet. He quickly retrieved a business card.

"So what can I do for you?" Jerry's tone was not friendly. It was obvious he was not pleased to have been interrupted from whatever it was he was doing.

"We have a problem." Dupree switched to his best litigator posture and tone.

"I don't remember ever meeting you," Jerry bristled.

"You haven't. You met my daughter Krista. We have a real problem." Dupree thrust out his business card.

Jerry looked down at the card, looked up and read the card again. "You don't look like no lawyer."

"That's because I'm on vacation. A vacation that was interrupted by my daughter's call for help. Now, Mister...?"

"Buckner," Jerry replied.

"Mr. Buckner. This shop doesn't look like it is worth all that much. I am presuming." Dupree paused for effect. "Isn't worth much at all. It is, from the looks of it, your sole source of income. Is that correct?"

"What does that matter?"

"I'll take that as a yes. Now, my daughter was humiliated and embarrassed by your suggestion she trade sexual favors for the work you did on her car. You made that obscene offer, I am certain, in front of my grandchildren."

"I didn't..." Jerry tried to show bravado but his voice gave him away.

"Now, now Mr. Buckner, Jerry, we both know that's not true. Here is my proposal. You tear up the bill, give me the keys to my daughter's car, and we get on with our lives."

"I'm not..."

"Yes you are," Dupree interrupted again. "Because if you don't I will bring a suit against you and your establishment that will be far more than the three hundred dollars you intended to charge her. You will lose the suit, and will not only have to pay your attorney, but you will have to pay court costs. The sexual harassment of the daughter of a highly-regarded Los Angeles attorney won't sit well with a judge, even here. Consider this, Jerry, she is a far more credible witness than you are."

"Now, now, I was just havin' a bit of fun. Just kiddin' around. Ya know?"

"I'm waiting for the keys, Mr. Buckner." Dupree had Jerry Buckner right where he wanted him. For the final blow, Dupree said, "It is a felony to give a false decline of a credit card. You really crossed the line there. I know for a fact her card has no limit." The bluff worked.

"Look mister, I don't want no trouble."

"Keys?"

Jerry disappeared in a heartbeat. Moments later a gray Volvo station wagon came around the side of the building.

With the motor still running, Jerry stepped out of the car. "Here you are. I don't want no trouble."

"This is the last you will hear from me, you have my word," Dupree said, walking to the car. He slipped into the driver's seat and did a U-turn out of the shallow driveway and back toward Smitty's.

As Dupree came back into the coffee shop, the waitress gave him a long unsmiling look. He just smiled and walked past her.

"How were the pancakes?" Dupree asked, sliding in next to Marcus.

"Yummy."

Dupree slid Krista's car keys across the table to her.

"Oh, that's wonderful! I promise to pay you back as soon as I get home. Honest, I will repay you, this is a miracle."

"There is nothing to pay back," Dupree said softly.

"I can't let you pay for the repairs, that's not fair."

"Like I told you, I made him an offer he couldn't refuse. He didn't charge you."

"I don't understand. You didn't hurt him, did you?"

Dupree let go a laugh and tried to answer, but it felt so good to laugh, he couldn't. "No, I would never hurt anyone. He wasn't willing to call my bluff. Smart move on his part. Anyway, you are all repaired and ready to be on your way."

"And you are going with us! That is the least I can do." Krista smiled broadly. "But I'm going to hold you to your promise to drive."

"I would expect nothing less."

At that moment, Dupree brushed his chin with his hand. He was more than a bit shocked to feel the stubble of whiskers. He has not missed a day of shaving since the day he passed the bar. Some days he shaved twice, morning before leaving for the office, and evening before going out to one function or another. He stroked his cheek and smiled.

"What's funny?" Krista asked.

"I just realized I haven't shaved in several days. I never skip shaving. It's like brushing my teeth. My room at the motel didn't have a mirror in the bathroom, just a piece of metal screwed to the wall. I didn't realize..." Dupree faded into a smile again.

"I thought you were going for the George Michael look."

"Who?"

"The singer? Never mind. Blast from the past."

Five minutes later, with kids secured in the back seat and Dupree's pack between his feet, the aging Volvo pulled out of Smitty's parking lot heading for Highway 99. Krista didn't look as they drove by Jerry's Transmissions, but Dupree did. Jerry was still standing in the big roll-up doorway. As the Volvo rolled by, Jerry defiantly raised his middle finger high in the air.

The highway was rough and bumpy. Potholes and truck ruts jarred and shook the car. NPR played softly on the radio until Merci started chanting Alvin! repeatedly. It seemed at first that Krista was ignoring her, focusing on her driving, passing the dozens of big trucks and dodging potholes. When Dupree thought he could bear the incessant demand for Alvin! no longer, Krista reached over and pushed a button on the stereo.

Merci squealed and her brother Marcus clapped excitedly as the thump-thump electronic beat was followed by the sound of the sped-up vocals of Alvin, Theodore, and Simon.

"They still make Chipmunk records?" Dupree asked in amazement.

"CDs? Yes they do, and they are a favorite with these two." Krista said, looking in the rear-view mirror.

Within minutes the socio-economic picture of Modesto changed dramatically. There were malls, restaurants, and names he recognized on businesses. Even the cars passing them were built in the twenty-first century.

"Look at that, a Holiday Inn!" Krista pointed.

"Slight upgrade from last night's accommodations, wouldn't you say?" Dupree chucked.

"Even that Super 8 Motel would have been twice as nice."

"I'm thirsty!" Marcus bellowed from the back seat.

"No, you're not. We just had breakfast and you drank lots of milk."

Out the window, the nicety of the mall and surrounding area gave way to farmland and industrial shop buildings.

"So, where are you coming from? I don't think I caught that part of the story." Dupree felt he was unnaturally loud to compensate for the music, singing, and clapping.

"Camp Pendleton. We did get interrupted a few times." Krista said pleasantly. "My husband Ezra's in Afghanistan, third tour. So, we are going home!" She pumped her fist with victorious glee.

"I'm hungry," Merci called out as the first song ended.

"No you're not, we just had breakfast," Krista replied over her shoulder.

"Do you have a lot of family in Idaho?" Dupree asked.

"Oh, yeah, five sisters and two brothers. I'm the kid in the middle. Tons of cousins too. Mom, dad, aunts, uncles, half the town is family. Then there are all the in-laws. Can't go anywhere without some relative or other being there. You really have to behave yourself!" Krista giggled. "So how about you? Lot of family?"

"No, not really. Both my parents are dead. I have some cousins but I don't have much contact with them."

"What about your wife?"

"She has a brother. We aren't very compatible."

"It must be lonely. No family to celebrate the holidays with," Krista offered.

"Can't miss what you never had," Dupree said solemnly.

What must be a favorite song brought wails of joy, and the loud singing began again, this time with the added irritation of Marcus kicking the back of Dupree's seat. The combination of the shrieking Chipmunks, combined with a toddler that didn't know the words, and a brother who punctuated the choruses with single word shouts of the lyrics, was giving Dupree tension in the back of his neck. He knew the signs; usually, it came from a client or opposing counsel in a deposition. A migraine would soon follow.

Dupree tried changing up his self-talk. The seat was comfortable. He felt safe. The company, minus the kids, was nice. He was assured of a nice long ride. It didn't help. The aura of a headache was beginning to flirt with the edges of his eyes.

"I got to go to the bathroom!" This time it was Marcus.

"Do you see a bathroom out here? You are just going to have to hold it until I see someplace to stop."

"That's funny!" Krista pointed at a road sign. "Manteca! That means lard in Spanish. Welcome to Lard!"

The kids, through all the racket, heard her comment and chimed in, first Marcus then Merci. They began to chant, "Welcome to Lard! Welcome to Lard! Welcome to Lard!"

Trying not to bring attention to himself, Dupree rubbed his temples. He felt like his head would explode. He had to get out of the car! The question was, how? Krista was a nice person, the kids were just kids, but he was years past the toddler and kindergarten age. He must come up with a plan. What was his reason? What was a reason to request he be put out? His thoughts were interrupted when the chant stopped and a plaintive cry cut through the music.

"I feel sick."

That was the only warning. The sound of retching and splashing vomit in the back seat only preceded the acrid stench by seconds. Krista turned in her seat and looked at Marcus just as he heaved another load of pancakes, milk, and last night's dinner onto the floor of the car.

"Oh, sweetie. Hold on, I'm pulling over." Krista signaled and pulled off onto the shoulder of the road.

The car barely came to a stop and Dupree's door was open and he leapt into the fresh air. He sucked in deep breaths of untainted air and let the cool wind soothe his face.

As Krista rounded the back of the car she called to Dupree, "Don't you go getting sick on me too!"

"I'm fine!" he called into the wind.

Cleaning the mess took nearly fifteen minutes. Marcus stood next to the side of the car, an ashen white. He threw up once more, then began the painful spasms of dry heaving. Dupree, for most of the time, leaned against the front of the car facing away from the clean-up. He did not feel compelled to assist or comfort the child.

"Must have been the milk hitting last night's hot dog from the Mini Mart. Good to go." Krista helped Marcus back into the car.

Dupree waited until she was in the car to get back in. The mess may have been mopped up in an old towel, but the smell remained. Dupree rolled down his window. The Chipmunks were silenced, and Merci whimpered softly as she sucked her thumb.

After about fifteen minutes, the first road sign announcing Stockton began to appear. This was the perfect opportunity for Dupree to make his escape. There were ten exits into the city of Stockton according to the sign. This was foreign territory and one exit was the same as the next to Dupree.

A new and very unfamiliar feeling overcame Dupree as he plotted his exit and tried to determine which exit was the best to request his departure. He was struggling with embarrassment, concern for Krista, and guilt at abandoning her. She was not his responsibility. He provided an escape from Modesto and the clutches of Jerry, the randy transmission man. He saved her a lot of money. They were strangers. Three hours ago, he knew nothing of her and her noisy, puking kids. His head pounded. For a man who heartlessly took people's houses, businesses, and represented the interests of legal, but ruthless, corporations for two decades, he found himself getting emotionally attached to this little family.

"Do you have a map?" Dupree asked.

"In the glove box. Why?"

"I'm sorry, but I just can't do this. I need you to let me off at the next exit." Dupree cleared his throat and opened the glove box. "I seem to recall that I-5 runs parallel to 99. It might be a better route for you to take."

"I don't understand. I thought you needed a ride to Oregon."

"Plans change," Dupree said coldly.

He found a map for Northern California. He ran his finger along Highway 99. "Yes, please take the Highway 4 exit, it will take you to I-5. I'll get out on one of the exits there."

"Alright." Krista's voice sounded concerned and confused.

The exit was a sharp incline on to a smooth new stretch of highway. They rode silently for several minutes.

"That one will work, please let me out there. Look, I'm sorry, but I guess I'm just too old to deal with little kids."

"They're just normal kids," Krista said defensively.

"I know, the problem lies with me. I appreciate the ride."

The exit went down into a dirty, rundown part of the city. Without a word, Krista pulled the car over.

"Thank you again. I hope you get to Idaho safe and sound. Good luck. Your husband is a lucky fellow." Dupree smiled, grabbed his pack, and opened the door.

"You didn't give that guy any money, did you?"

"No, I didn't. We just had a talk." Dupree stepped from the car and closed the door.

Chapter 5

To the north of where Dupree stood was a street of old bars, liquor stores, and the darkened spaces of closed businesses. This is not going to work, he thought, as he walked in the sunshine. He was standing in a Skid Row area that was as bad as anything in L.A. The whole place made the ratty area of Modesto that Dupree walked along this morning look like the playground at McDonald's. The number of derelicts was astounding. Groups of black men gathered on corners and in the doorways of low rent hotels. Large numbers of Mexicans leaned against the windows and walls of old abandoned stores and restaurants. They smoked and passed bottles in brown paper bags. Some didn't bother with the bag.

All along the chain-link fences that bordered the exit were makeshift, homeless shelters of cardboard boxes and black plastic. Blankets and plastic tarps covered frameworks of shopping carts, plywood, and plastic milk crates. People were bundled in filthy blankets and the occasional sleeping bag. Several dogs slept curled up next to their masters. Even in the cool breeze sweeping through the covering of the overpass, the stench of human waste cut through.

Dupree continued his survey of the area. To the south was mostly concrete, gray warehouses, and industrial business. As the light changed just beyond the overpass, a black and white police cruiser rounded the corner. As it approached him, he raised his arm to flag it down.

"Good afternoon," the young Hispanic officer said, rolling down his window.

"Hi. I seem to have wandered into a pretty questionable neighborhood."

"You could say that for sure." The officer chuckled and turned to his partner. "I've heard it called a lot of things, but questionable is a new one. What can we do for you?"

"How far is it to civilization?"

"At least a mile to get out of this mess."

"Are there taxis?"

"Where are you from? No sane cabbie would come down here."

"Los Angeles. So, can you point me in the safest direction?"

"I can do better than that. In the interest of public safety..."

"He means yours," the officer in the passenger seat interrupted.

"Yeah, that's what I meant, your safety and well-being, as a visitor to our fair city. If you don't mind hopping in the back, we'll get you to safety. We are about to go off duty."

The passenger-side officer got out, rounded the back of the car and opened the back door.

"I'm going to pat you down. It is for our safety and yours. Just procedure. Please put your hands on top of the car." The officer moved quickly and methodically. "All done. Thanks."

"Very enlightening." Dupree smiled. No civil case there, he thought.

"We'll let you off just a little ways from the station. Buses and taxis are available there. Be sure and use a yellow cab that says City Taxi." The radio under the dash squawked. "Not for us, I'm going home. So what brings you to Stockton?"

"I'm on my way to Washington and got sidetracked with a bit of car trouble," Dupree said through the steel mesh screen that divided them. "My ride dropped me off at the wrong exit. I'm glad you fellas came along. I was a bit out of my element back there."

"Me too," the cop in the passenger seat chimed in.

"Well, this will be a lot better place to arrange where you're going." The patrol car pulled over.

Dupree reached for the door handle.

The officer in the passenger seat watched as he felt around the door. "Not going to find it!" The officer said good-heartedly. "Hold on, I'll let you out."

"I've never been in the back of a patrol car before."

"That's what I figured," the officer said, as the door swung open.

"Thank you so much for the ride," Dupree said, stepping onto the curb.

"To serve and protect," the driver said out his window.

The patrol car pulled away, and Dupree took in his surroundings: Pizza Hut, Wendy's, a car wash, and a lot of average looking citizens. Breakfast seemed a long time ago so Dupree made his way toward Wendy's. He was hungry, but the thought of something heavy in his stomach didn't seem to appeal. As he read the menu, the idea of a chocolate Frosty sounded like just the thing.

An older couple, perhaps in their late seventies, made their way across the dining room and sat in the booth next to Dupree. From the start, he could tell they were losing their hearing. Not that they were shouting, but their voices were elevated just enough for Dupree to hear every word as if he were sitting with them.

"Did you want more ketchup?" the man asked, as they settled in the seats.

"No dear, this will be fine," his wife replied.

The couple sat quietly eating their lunch, as Dupree wondered what it must be like to be with someone for so long. He dreamed of falling in love with his soulmate when he was young and dying in each other's arms at an old age. His wife certainly wasn't his soulmate. He heard a lot about soulmates in his Literature classes, and around tables at smoky late-night, wine-fueled, philosophical discussions, and it always sounded like that person was out there somewhere. Then again, books, music, and film are filled with the ones that got away or were lost in some tragic romantic way. It never happened to Dupree.

He met his wife in an Art History class. He was in the last year of his undergraduate work. His law school was set, his path lay before him. The chart he made of his five, ten and twenty-year goals were xeroxed and taped in the front of all his textbooks, on his mirror, and the dashboard of his car. Nothing would deter him from those goals.

Number three on the list of five-year goals was a beautiful wife, good hostess, a good networker, social climber, and an asset to his outside life with the firm. Nothing was said of love, soulmates, or long term, lasting relationships. Toward the bottom of the list was 2.5 children. They were seen as part of the formula, not something to be longed for, desired, or anticipated. Much like making partner on or before year ten of the goals, they were a puzzle piece.

Dupree couldn't imagine sitting in a fast-food restaurant with his wife, not now or in forty years. What was it that drew him to her? He imagined he was back in his Art History class twenty-some years ago. She sat four rows in front of him in the large lecture hall. He noticed her on the first day. Long legs, great butt, flaxen hair, and a backpack with patches from European cities and countries.

As the days went by Dupree methodically inched up closer to her. Finally, he was directly behind her. He waited each day as she seemed to glide into the row, pull a yellow notepad from her backpack, and settle in for the lecture. She was actually interested. To Dupree, the class was just three credits of required Fine Arts.

The second day sitting behind her he offered her a warm smile and a friendly, "Good Morning."

She smiled and nodded.

This went on for three more class meetings before he worked up the nerve to walk up the aisle beside her after class. He offered a cheerful, "Have a great day!" as he turned left and she went right.

Two more cheerful partings, and then he turned right as well. Idle chatter turned to asking her for coffee, then a movie, and the hook was set. Dupree, in his logical, practical, goal-driven way, decided she passed the audition. He would marry her after he passed the bar. She never knew she was part of the plan; she thought it was love.

Diane was a good country club name. He liked her, actually quite a lot. Was it love? Dupree thought maybe it was, but he had no feeling to compare it with, no point of reference, so he settled for whatever the feeling was. Over the years, the 'a lot' was dropped. A few years after that like seemed a foreign concept for the woman he shared his bed with, had sex with—he never thought of it as making love—conceived children with, and occupied a four thousand square foot house with. Tolerated, perhaps was a better word. Now, even that no longer applied.

The Frosty was gone far too quickly. Dupree stood and started to leave, then turned back to the table where the elderly couple sat.

"Pardon me, but can I ask you folks a question?"

"I suppose so, 'less it's for money." The old man smiled.

"No, it's not that," Dupree continued. "How many years have you been married?"

"Al," the woman said grinning.

"Fifty-eight years. That right?"

His wife beamed as she nodded her head. "That's right."

"I have to ask. What your secret?"

"Have a seat and I'll tell you all about it," Al said.

"Yes, please join us. I'm Sylvia." Her hand shot out at Dupree, and he was taken aback by her firm grip.

"I'm Dupree."

Al slid over making room on the seat.

"The secret to a strong, long, marriage is marrying your best friend. That way you never run out of stuff to talk about or wonder what they're up to. It's always a pleasure to be together. Remember the small stuff don't matter, and the big stuff is dealt with together."

"And never go to bed angry," Sylvia added.

"It seems I missed the boat from the start," Dupree said, as much to himself as Al and Sylvia.

"Now, that is a shame. Never too late to try again."

"What about love? You didn't mention love," Dupree pressed.

"Well, of course we love each other, silly," Sylvia began. "There are different kinds of love. There's that fluttery young love, there's can't keep your hands off each other love, there's hurt when they hurt love, there's hold their head when they're pukin' with the flu love. The most important is the kind you don't talk about much. It's the, I will never leave you, love. At our age, that's the deepest, realest of all. Because we know we only got a few more years on this old earth.

No one wants to go first because we can't stand the thought of leavin' the other alone. Seems like a lie if you die first, you know what I mean."

"I believe I do," Dupree replied.

"She leave ya?" Al asked.

"No, no, nothing like that." Dupree chuckled. "Nothing like that." Dupree stood. "Thanks, I never had the opportunity to ask anyone together for a long time. I think you two are very special. Thank you."

"I hope you find someone to love," Sylvia said, as Dupree walked away.

He stopped, and for a long moment considered what the old lady just said. Is that what this was about? He needed someone to love? God knows there is no one on earth he cared about, let alone loved. Did he already know the answer when he sat down? He turned slowly and looked back at the old couple. They were back in deep conversation. Sylvia looked up, saw Dupree, and winked. He smiled and made his way to the door.

Back on the sidewalk, Dupree looked around for a sign indicating a freeway. There was nothing. A few yards to his right two kids were sitting on a bus bench.

"Where's this bus go?" Dupree inquired.

"Home." A thin, pimple-faced redhead in a Delta College sweatshirt said with self-amusement.

"I asked for that," Dupree said good-heartedly. "All points east."

"Freeway?"

"I-5 I suppose. I don't really know. I just started school here. I'm from Washington."

"State?" Dupree asked.

"Yes, sir."

"Let me ask you something. Do you know of a small town there, maybe in the mountains, lots of trees, friendly people?"

"White Owl. Full of artsy types and old hippies, lots of live music. They have a festival there I think. You know tie-dye, organic farms, handcrafts, cool place to visit. I went there once on the way to meet some friends for a backpacking trip."

"How about to live?"

"You don't look like the hippie type. But yeah, it would be cool, I think." Pimples looked up at the approaching bus. "Here we go," he said to the other kid on the bench whose eyes were closed.

"Thanks for the info." Dupree offered.

"This bus doesn't go there though." Pimples laughed.

The bus brakes whooshed and the doors opened. The two boys hopped on the bus.

Dupree took the first step onto the bus. "How close do you get to the freeway?"

" 'Bout a hundred yards." The driver replied.

Dupree took another step up.

"Eighty-five cents."

Dupree paid and looked around. There were only about a dozen people on the bus. He took a seat behind the driver. The ride was pleasant enough. The bus rolled past a park, a few old houses, and a lot of businesses. Ten minutes later the bus came to a stop between Burger King and McDonald's.

"End of the line. Transfers at the bench. Everybody off," the driver said into the microphone.

Dupree was the first one off the bus. Just like the driver said, a freeway entrance sign marked the north ramp to Interstate 5.

Pack in hand, Dupree stationed himself on the sidewalk outside the Burger King's chain link fence and under the shade of a low hanging tree. He stuck his thumb out and waited for a ride.

Most cars not only didn't slow down, but they also sped up as they turned the corner onto the northbound ramp. He tried his best to smile and make eye contact but after an hour, the smile was feeling plastic and forced. After two hours, the smile was gone. He tried at least to look cheerful and nonthreatening but he was beginning to mutter under his breath.

Three hours of standing and waiting for a ride set a new record. Dupree was in full frustration mode and called the drivers of cars a variety of creative names as they roared by.

At three hours and twelve minutes, a mid-nineties, navy blue Mustang slowly approached. The paint was worn off every leading surface like it drove for miles through a sand storm. It rolled to a slow stop in front of Dupree.

"Where you headed?" the driver asked through a half rolled down window.

"Washington."

"I'm only going as far as Redding, but you're welcome to come along if you want."

"Sounds great, thanks." Dupree opened the door and got in.

The car sped away and onto the freeway. The first thing Dupree noticed was the amount of trash inside the car. The back seat literally looked like the driver threw fast-food sacks and cups over his shoulder. Beer cans punctuated the refuse.

"I'm Dupree."

"Cutter." The name wasn't followed with any further comment.

As Dupree settled in for hopefully a long ride, he realized he had no idea where Redding was. He grinned to himself. His comfort zone was, little by little, shredding like an old flag in the wind. The trash in the car extended to the floor around Dupree's feet and he tried to push it aside enough to find a place for his feet and pack to comfortably rest.

"You can throw that shit in the back with all the rest. Didn't know I was having company."

Dupree grabbed several handfuls of trash and placed it on the mess in the back seat. "That's better," Dupree said cheerfully.

He got no response. There was a pungent odor in the car. It wasn't spoiled food or body odor, more like the lingering scent of skunk. He dismissed it. The smell was bearable, and not a reason to complain after three hours waiting for a ride. Still, he wondered what it was.

The car rode in the middle lane, occasionally passing slower cars, but always on the right, never into the fast lane. Dupree glanced at the speedometer as they passed a road sign announcing Lodi. The car was sailing along at well over eighty miles an hour.

"You smoke?" Cutter asked.

"No."

"Good, I hate to share." Cutter laughed and pulled a small plastic-tipped cigar out of his shirt pocket. "I pack these blunts myself."

"Blunt?"

"Yeah, I buy Black and Tan cigars, split 'em open long ways, remove the guts and stuff 'em with weed. Then close 'em back up. Makes for a smooth smoke, nobody knows what you got, and they light easy. Greatest invention ever."

Dupree knew, or figured, that his son was probably a regular user of marijuana. In the last few years, he was around him so little Dupree really didn't have any firm evidence, but his slovenly ways and total lack of motivation were a pretty good indication. The smell was so far in his past that Dupree really didn't remember it until Cutter lit up. The car filled quickly with the pungent smoke. Dupree cracked the window. Cutter inhaled so deeply Dupree thought it must reach his toes.

"Sure you don't want a hit?"

"No, I'm good."

Cutter continued to smoke, and Dupree noticed a considerable reduction in speed.

"You know anything about The Urantia Book? You look like a pretty smart guy," Cutter asked as he took another deep lung full of smoke.

"No, can't say that I do. What is it?"

Cutter raised his index finger, signaling Dupree that he wanted to hold the smoke as long as possible. "Whoa," he said, finally exhaling. "It's a book and a place. I've been reading it. It is full of all kinds of wisdom, truth, and spiritual guidance."

"Like a Bible?"

"It is like the fifth revelation. You know, like a sacred handing down of knowledge."

"Who wrote it?" Dupree inquired.

"Oh, nobody knows, but it is controlled by The Forum, or at least it was until the powerful forces of organized religion tried to destroy the book. They stole the copyright so the sacred leaders couldn't sell the book to finance the spreading of the word. But there are lots of followers. I mean I've only met a couple, but in the east there are lots."

"Funny, I missed that one. So it is a book and a place?" Dupree was sure this was the stoned babblings of a pothead, but he decided to play along.

"Urantia is located in a universe called Nebadon, it's in Orvonton universe which is part of Super Universe Number Seven."

"You seem to have studied it a lot." Dupree tried to not let his amusement show.

"I think I might be destined to fuse with my divine fragment and become one inseparable entity with it. Becoming a Finaliter is my real goal."

"A what?"

"A Finaliter. It's a person who continues their spiritual journey as an ascending citizen of the universe. They like to travel through all kinds of worlds on a long pilgrimage to grow and learn. The thing is, it eventually leads to God and you become one of the Paradise Mortals.

"But I have to find my Thought Adjuster, to guide me toward an increased understanding of him. There are things that aren't revealed to me yet, like the Isle of Paradise where God lives, right? This is what is kind of blurry to me, Paradise is surrounded by Havona, kind of an eternal universe containing a billion perfect worlds. Now, around them, seven incomplete and evolutionary Super Universes circle. That there is some trippy shit I just can't get ahold of.

"The Bible stuff is way more clearer. Did you know that Jesus' crucifixion was the outcome of religious leaders back in the day who thought that Jesus' teaching was a threat to their being in charge of stuff? See, the church today has got it all wrong, Jesus was actually the human incarnation of Michael of Nebadon, one of more than 700,000 Paradise Sons of God. There is just so much we are never taught.

"Did you know Jimi Hendrix carried the Book of Urantia? He said it was an alternative Bible. He carried it with him everywhere, that and his Bob Dylan songbook. Cool or what? That's your generation, right? Hendrix and Dylan?"

"So they say," Dupree shrugged. "How did you come upon this book of Ur..."

"Urantia. A dude that sold my friend Ricky PCP was friends with this girl that was always hooking up with this old guy, kind of a Manson kinda freak, scary as hell. Well, he gave a copy to Ricky's cousin. Ricky owed me money so he gave me the book. He said it was kind of a Jack and the Beanstalk kinda trade. I was really stoned one night, I mean higher than a moonbat at harvest time, you know, so I started reading it and it was like a window to God opened up. I knew right then I needed to listen to what it was teaching."

"Wow."

"Right? You feel me?"

"I think I do," was the only thing Dupree could think of to say. He was beginning to feel a little funny. Oddly enough, Cutter's rambling was starting to make sense. The closed space and the incredible amount of smoke in the car might just be affecting him. Is this what it is to get high? he thought. He rolled the window the rest of the way down.

"Okay, Okay, Okay, I got to think now. Hold on, hold on. I always get confused right in here. All these exits and bypasses and signs mess me up. This is Sacramento, right?"

"That's what the signs say," Dupree answered.

"Okay, Okay, so Redding sign? You see it?" Cutter was frantic.

"Yeah, there!" Dupree pointed to the far-left lanes.

Cutter didn't signal or look, he just started to drift in the direction of the lane with Redding overhead. Horns blared, a car swerved and brakes screamed. Cutter didn't flinch or change expression. He crossed four lanes of the freeway at fifty miles an hour while the cars flew past and around him at seventy or above. Dupree held onto the dashboard and prayed. To whom, he wasn't sure.

"Okay, we're cool now," Cutter said flatly.

A black SUV pulled alongside them and a man screaming, swearing, and half hanging out the window gave Cutter the finger.

"What's his trip?" Cutter asked indignantly.

"I think you may have cut him off changing lanes," Dupree offered.

"No way! Really?"

"Could be."

Cutter flashed a peace sign at the man in the SUV as it sped away. He took another long draw from his blunt and frowned. "You know it is this whole Illuminati thing. They are taking over the world little by little. Sneaky, subtle ways. Creeping into everything."

"I have to get out more. I have gotten a real education since I got in your car. I have never heard of the Illuminati. Is it part of Urantia?" Dupree was kind of enjoying stringing Cutter along. It certainly made the time go by faster.

"Whoa, I never thought of that. Could be, could be. You are one insightful dude. Are you a searcher too?"

"Not exactly." Dupree left it at that. "So where is Illuminati? Italy?"

"No, no man, it is a secret society going all the way back to Cain and Abel.

"Here's what's up, there really are only two religions in the world. Those who worship God and those who don't, right? So really, if you think about it, if you're not on God's team, you are already on Satan's. It's like Dylan said, 'It might be the devil or it may be the Lord, but you're gonna have to serve somebody.'

"So, the Illuminati is this secret society that's way above all organized religion and political parties, its thing is to unite the world in allegiance to the devil. To rule the world for Satan.

"So get this, there are all kinds of presidents going way, way back that are members of the Illuminati. Popes are big-time involved. Entertainers too, man, Jay-Z and Beyoncé are the full-on ambassadors to the young people of the world. And, who's their best buddy? B-rock O!"

"That is quite a bit to swallow," Dupree said, in the pause.

"I know, right? But get this, it goes back, man. They love to hide their symbolism in plain sight. It is how they recognize each other. The initiated aren't afraid to put it right out there because the unenlightened don't get it anyway.

"Like the pentagram, right? The upside-down star?"

"Yes, I know what a pentagram is," Dupree confirmed.

"That demonic goat god that the Illuminati idolize? The heavy metal duds stole it, but they aren't really Illuminati, they're just poseurs. The real ones are like everywhere once you know where to look, like on money, Catholic churches, all kinds of stuff. Oh, and you know this?" Cutter held up his hand, his index and little fingers extended, his thumb holding down the other two. "Heavy metal, right? Wrong, dude. Ancient symbol for devil horns. Scary, huh? But the really trippy one is this!" He made an A-OK sign and held it up to his eye. "That's the big one!"

"Alright, I know this one. We did it at summer camp." Dupree made two of the hand gestures and put them up to his eyes upside down. "Up in the air junior birdmen, up in the air upside down," he began to sing.

"No, no, no Dude! The three fingers sticking out? 666 the number of the Beast. The thing around the eyes, the third eyes, all-seeing like on the pyramid on the dollar bill. There's all kinds of famous people in pictures doing it. It is a signal to the devil, kind of a wink and a thank you for the power you've given me."

"Like who?" Dupree asked, skeptically.

"Shit, I don't know, let's see. The Pope, Prince Charles, Lady Ga-Ga, all kinds of people. But that ain't all. Masonic stuff like the ruler and triangle thing, that ain't got nothin' to do with bricks, I can tell you that. That's one.

"There's a ton of other symbols to show they're in charge. You know that tower kinda thing, like the Washington Monument with the pyramid on top? Those things are all over the world, man. So are serpents and dragons. Symbols. The All-Seeing Eye, like on the dollar bill. It's all around too, once you start to look. Even owls show up as Illuminati symbols. Yeah, can you say Harry Potter? I tell you, man, they are everywhere.

"I wish I had a computer to show you all the famous people in the Illuminati. You know who else is into this shit big time? Mormons, man. In Salt Lake City I saw it, all over their big ol' temple. Cray-zee!" Cutter rolled down the window and threw the last inch of the cigar and the plastic tip out.

"Arbuckle." Dupree pointed at the road sign. "Did you know one of the biggest scandals of the twentieth century involved a guy named Arbuckle?" Dupree was not much for trivia, but in law school, he was assigned the task of defending Fatty Arbuckle in his famous trial.

"Yeah? What'd they do?" Cutter asked.

"Fatty Arbuckle was just about the most famous movie star in the world in the era of silent movies. Before sound, comedy was king, because it didn't require dialog, just a lot of physical gags. Slapstick is what they called it. Anyway, Mr. Arbuckle attended a pretty rowdy party at the St. Francis Hotel in San Francisco. A young woman named Virginia Rappe was allegedly sexually assaulted with a champagne bottle. The point is, there was no evidence that Mr. Arbuckle had anything to do with it. He was exonerated, but it ruined his career none the less. A very sad affair."

"You know what?" Cutter began. "You talk just like a lawyer."

"I watch a lot of TV." Dupree tried to deflect the compliment. He certainly didn't want to tell his driver he was indeed an attorney.

"Yeah, but you sound like you know what you're talking about. You got a lot of school?"

"I went to college." Dupree nodded. "You explained the incredibly complicated path of your philosophy pretty well. What college did you go to?"

"No college for me. I didn't even finish high school. I thought it meant getting high so I graduated with a diploma in weed." Cutter laughed as if he told the funniest joke in the world. He coughed and sputtered and leaned over the steering wheel. "Oh man, I'm runnin' out of gas."

"The sign back there a bit said Williams was fifteen miles," Dupree offered.

"Ass, grass, or gas. Nobody rides for free. How much money do you have?"

"About forty or fifty bucks. How much do you want?" Dupree saw the driver pull a pistol out from under his right thigh.

"Forty or fifty bucks."

"Whoa, let's not get excited."

"I'm not excited at all. I'm feeling pretty well baked," Cutter said, pulling over to the side of the road.

"Alright, alright." Dupree unbuckled his seat belt and tried to get his hand into his pocket.

"What's in the pack?"

"Dirty underwear, a Bible, and a toy for my grandson." Dupree huffed trying to lean back far enough to get his hands in his pocket. If he weren't so scared, he would have grinned at his ability to lie under pressure.

After nearly bending over the seat backward Dupree managed to get the small wad of bills from his pocket. He unfolded them and began to count.

"No need for that. Hand it over."

"That's all I have to get me to Washington!" Dupree protested.

In a powerful arc of his arm, Cutter slammed Dupree across the bridge of his nose with the underside of the gun. His vision exploded in a blinding burst of white light, then darkness. Dupree was sure he blacked out because the next thing he knew his door was open and Cutter was sitting sideways in the seat pushing him out with the bottom of his boots. In a last moment of clarity, Dupree clutched the strap of his pack as he fell from the car.

"Later Dude!"

A moment later the car lurched forward throwing dirt and gravel in its wake. Dupree blinked several times and let the heaviness of his eyelids overtake him.

Chapter 6

"Hey! Hey, Buddy! You okay?"

The sharp gravel cut into Dupree's palms and knees but it wasn't enough to clear his head. He looked around for the owner of the voice. The roar he thought was in his head was, in reality, the mufflerless engine of a three-wheel ATV that pulled up alongside the ditch next to him.

"You need some help?"

"I think so." Dupree's voice sounded to him like it was coming out of someone else.

As he lifted his head, he saw two legs clothed in very faded denim and a pair of partially laced work boots. He felt the grip of a strong pair of hands grasp his shoulders and gently begin to lift him.

"Can you make it to your feet?"

"I think so," Dupree said, struggling to put his weight on the soles of his feet.

As Dupree stood to his feet, he was looking into the weathered, deeply creased face of the owner of the ATV.

"You get hit by a car?"

"No, I believe the term is pistol-whipped."

"Hell of a blow you took. Can you make it to the trailer?"

"I believe so," Dupree said, softer than he intended.

"Let's give it a try. We need to get you some medical attention."

"My pack." Dupree's voice was getting back to normal, but it carried a thick nasal quality. "I need my pack."

"Alright, I'll grab it. Let's get you in the trailer first."

The man took Dupree by the top of his arm and directed him toward the little green trailer behind the ATV.

"Watch your step," the man said as they approached the ditch. "There you go. I gotcha."

Dupree turned and sat on the end of the trailer. He turned his head from side to side and then leaned it way back to look straight up to the sky. His neck popped and crackled, and the short, sharp pain was a relief. He took a deep breath and looked back at the man who was retrieving his backpack.

The man was either much younger than he looked or much more agile than a man his age should be. Obviously a farmer. Dupree wondered what profit there could be in owning a piece of this desolate expanse of dry weeds and rock.

"There you are." The man handed Dupree his pack. "I'm Chet Weaver. My house is about three-quarters of a mile off. Try to get comfy, it'll be kind of bumpy in spots."

"Thank you for coming to my rescue."

"You're lucky, I usually don't make it this far out until Wednesday." Chet gave Dupree a broad smile.

"Lucky must be a two-edged sword. I'm Dupree."

"Nice to meet you. The circumstances could be better." Chet took a radio from his belt and keyed the microphone. "Val? You there?"

The radio's static was thick and hurt Dupree's head.

"I'm here," a woman's voice said on the other end of the radio.

"I just found a fella who's got a nasty cut across the bridge of his nose. Better get your kit out. I'm at marker 109 so I'll be a bit."

"I'll be ready. You be careful." The voice was halting and slurred.

"See you in a bit," Chet replied. "Hang tight."

The pop, pop, pop of the ATV provided a warning for the hard-jerking start. Dupree held on with a tight grasp as they started off. The little trailer bumped hard, then smoothed a bit as they headed east away from the highway.

Dupree tried several times to close his eyes and relax, but the jolts and bumps of the well-worn dirt path seemed to send sharp pains up his back that exploded out the bridge of his nose. The landscape grew no greener or any more promising as they rode along. There was neither tree nor brush as far as he could see. Riding backward kept Dupree from seeing the approaching farmhouse until they turned and rolled onto the smooth paved driveway.

The house and yard were an oasis in the parched desolation of the surroundings. Broad branched fruitless mulberry trees surrounded the house and their broad leaves offered shade and a protective break from the wind. Grass as thick and green as any golf course wrapped itself around the house. Under the wide front porch were flowerbeds of bright yellow daisies that welcomed you to the front steps.

Chet stopped with Dupree and the trailer right at the front steps. A tall slender woman stood on the porch with her arms folded across her chest. Her face was lovely, olive-complected, and void of the weathered ravages Chet exhibited. Her hair was pulled back in a ponytail and was dark with broad stripes of white. The dark blue dress she wore clung to her youthful figure. Dupree found her overall appearance quite pleasing.

"Valericia, this is Mr. Dupree," Chet offered, giving a nod of the head to his passenger.

The woman eyed Dupree suspiciously, then gave him a grudging hint of a smile. "'Ullo."

Chet rounded the trailer and offered Dupree a helping hand, which he declined. Dupree used the handrail to help him up the five steps to the porch.

Dupree offered Valericia his hand, she did not unfold her arms, just turned and walked to the front door.

"Don't mind her. She's just leery of strangers. She was an RN, she'll fix you right up."

As he entered the house Dupree was surprised at the décor. It was surprisingly modern and accented with several pieces of abstract art, not at all what he would have expected in a hundred-year-old farmhouse. The living room was bright and cheerful. A large bouquet of blown glass flowers sat atop a sharp-angled glass table. Dupree followed Valericia into what he expected to be the kitchen. Instead, it was a studio of sorts. There were several easel paintings in various stages of completion. What looked to be a glass cutting table and two large tanks with copper torch heads stood against a tiled wall.

A tall wooden stool stood near the wall to his right. "Sit." Valericia indicated the stool.

The dull throbbing in his head seemed to be receding. His thought process was back, and the haze of the blow and being ejected from the car were all but gone. Dupree was surprised at the amount of blood he saw when he looked down at the front of his shirt. What did he expect? The sight of the red stain reinforced the severity of his injury.

"I certainly appreciate your kindness. I hope I'm not too big an imposition."

Dupree tried to muster a smile.

"She's happy to help, aren't you?" Chet said, not really expecting an answer.

The cupboard door was open and Valericia pulled out a bottle of alcohol and clean cotton cloth. Above the cupboard was a small counter and on it sat a bowl of steaming water, a group of serious-looking tools, and two packages Dupree couldn't identify.

As Valericia began to gently wipe Dupree's upper lip and chin of dried blood, he detected a slight lack of symmetry in what he thought such a pretty face. The corner of her right eye and mouth drooped ever so slightly when she relaxed, which wasn't often.

"'Urt a bit?" she asked softly as she touched his nose for the first time. She squeezed the cloth and let warm water flood the wound. "Broken."

"You think so?" Chet asked as he approached where Dupree sat. "Let me take a look." As Chet looked closely at Dupree, he saw for the first time, the dark bruises beginning to form around his eyes. With the blood mostly washed away, the depth of the gash across Dupree's nose was clearly apparent. "Do you mind?"

Chet gently felt the sides of Dupree's nose. "Yep, broken alright. You ever broke your nose before?" Chet ran his finger across Dupree's brow, then back to his nose. I broke mine half a dozen times playing football.

Ever so gently, Chet placed his index and middle finger on either side of Dupree's nose. Without warning or pausing in his description of his football years, he twisted Dupree's nose with a hard, rapid right and then immediately left. Dupree shot straight up from the stool and gave a resounding expletive and a deep throaty "argh."

"Hurts so good, right?" Chet asked.

"What the hell did you do?" Dupree asked in disbelief.

"I just snapped her back. Kind of like popping your knuckles, huh?"

"Not really." Dupree blew out in a huge sigh. "But you're right, it was like having your back pop back into place. It hurts kind of but in a good way."

"Exactly." Chet smiled.

Dupree looked at Valericia for the first time. She was grinning from ear to ear. The effects of her paralysis were more pronounced than ever, but somehow it diminished her beauty little.

"Saw-ree," Valericia began, "Good cop, bad cop."

Chet laughed heartily. "She's grouchy and I'm Mr. Trustworthy so you never see it coming. I doubt you'd ever let her put you back in place. We used to play that one with our kids."

"No, it would've sounded just too painful. Crazy as it sounds, it doesn't hurt anymore."

"Works every time," Chet assured.

Valericia stepped over to Dupree and guided him back to the stool. "We fix cut now. It 'urt a bit." She removed two butterfly strips from their packaging and one at a time used them to pull the wound together creating an X between Dupree's eyes.

Valericia placed her hand on Dupree's cheek and said, "All done."

"We need to give him a couple of aspirin."

"Come." Valericia indicated the door with a jerk of her head.

As she walked away, Dupree saw a slight limp in her right leg. He followed obediently, once again trying to take in the different artistic mediums across the room. At the doorway, they turned right into a short hallway and into the kitchen.

"Have a seat," Chet said from behind. "Coffee, tea, or something stronger?"

"Tea sounds good." Dupree took a chair.

"Now, you're going to need to blow out the clots. So, if you feel like you need to blow, do it. Sooner the better, the tea will help loosen things up." Chet tossed a roll of paper towels on the table.

Valericia placed two pills in front of Dupree. "Ass-pur-in," she said slowly. Turning, she took a glass of water from the counter and handed it to Dupree.

"Vallie had a stroke three years ago. I was afraid I was going to lose her. But, she's come back with flying colors. Thankfully, it really only affected her speech. They said at first she wouldn't be able to walk or work her hands. But God was with us, and she gets around without any problems. Piss her off and you'll see, she can still yell with the best of them." Chet laughed merrily.

"Stop." Valericia waggled her finger at Chet. "I don't yell."

There was a long break in the conversation. Dupree caught Chet glancing at Valericia, and she gave him a go on kind of look. Chet moved towards the stove, where he waited for the kettle to boil.

"You seem like a pretty nice guy." Chet cleared his throat nervously. "What happened to put you on the side of the road with your nose bashed in?"

"Fair question. First, though, I want to thank you for taking me in and mending me. Not a lot of people would have. I am grateful." Dupree looked from one of his hosts to the other. "I was in Stockton and hitched a ride with this guy named Cutter. At first, I just thought he was some stoner goofball. He had all kinds of weird religious beliefs if you could call them that, and some really ridiculous conspiracy theories.

"He smoked a cigar stuffed full of marijuana, and I figured he was harmless. That was until he demanded money for gas. I offered, but he wanted all I had. That's when he pulled his pistol. I guess I didn't hand it over fast enough, and he clubbed me with it, kicked me, I mean, literally kicked me with both feet from the car, and that's where you come in." Dupree grimaced as he smiled and shrugged his shoulders.

"You know, Mister Dupree..."

"Just Dupree, please."

"Alright. I've seen a lot of hitchhikers in my day. I've lived here all my life so that's quite a few years of bums, soldiers, and hippies with their thumb out. Frankly, you don't fit the mold. Now, why don't you tell us what is really going on? You don't look or speak the part you are trying to play. You're safe here. You're not armed, or I don't think that guy could have got the drop on you." Chet gave Dupree an upward jerk of his head. "What's going on?"

"You've got a very perceptive eye, my friend. Of course, you're right. This is the first time I ever hitchhiked in my life." Dupree gave a soft chuckle. "I am, was, an attorney from Southern California. I got up a couple of days ago and realized I hated my life, wife, and kids. Have you ever wanted to just disappear and make a new start? I seriously contemplated killing myself, but that wouldn't solve my problem, just end it with no benefit. So, I was driving to work and decided to turn left instead of right."

"Just like that."

"Just like that." Dupree put his hands up in surrender.

At that moment, the kettle began to whistle. Valericia sat quietly studying Dupree and Chet got up to get the kettle. No one spoke as Chet put three mugs on the table with teabag tags dangling from them. He poured the steaming water in each cup, returned the kettle to the stove, and returned with three spoons and a sugar bowl.

"Sugar?"

"Yes?" Valericia said coyly.

The three laughed, relieving the tension.

"To be honest, the only time I ever considered running off was when I thought I was going to get drafted," Chet explained. "I was going to be Canada bound. Then I got my acceptance letter to UC Davis and a college deferment. My course was set from that day on. I didn't know it, but it was about to get real good!"

Valericia slapped Chet's arm playfully. "He mean he met me."

"That is the truth. We both went to Davis. I was a full-blown Aggie and Val was studying biology. She planned to be a doctor."

"Too hard," she interrupted. "So, I became a nurse."

"Cheater, you're getting ahead of the story. Second year there, I was enrolled in a physiology class. Hardest class I was ever in. The prof asked if there was anyone who would like to help him organize study groups."

"That's me! Extra credits!" Valericia giggled girlishly.

"Somehow I ended up in her study group." Chet smiled at his wife.

"I did that too! He was cute," she stammered.

"If you can imagine such a thing, as pretty as she is now, she was even prettier then!"

"Funny." Valericia beamed.

The love these two showed for each other pained Dupree. He wanted to celebrate with them, be happy and excited over the love they have shared for so many years, but it made his heart ache. He guessed it was jealousy.

"Something tells me our story isn't sitting so well with you," Chet said softly.

"No, it is just something I never had. I guess in a way I'm jealous. Please go on, I'm enjoying the story, really."

"We got engaged senior year. The only problem was she had to go home. Not just to another state, but Argentina. As a graduation gift, my folks gave me a ticket to go and visit her parents. Here's a funny. I was so proud of this land and that my great-grandfather settled it, and my grandfather and my dad worked it, that I talked about it a lot. One day I was going on and on. That was the day that this one tells me her folks are ranchers. Well, of course I got all excited. So, I told her we had five hundred acres and asked how many they had."

"Please, not so nice," Valericia cut in.

Chet paused for a moment, "She did this cute little giggle and said they had twenty-five thousand acres! I asked what they farmed, she said, 'No farm, ranch. We raise cattle.' I did what any Aggie worth their salt would do. Stupid me, I just had to ask how many." Chet laughed. "She said there were too many to count!"

"I was not bragging, jus' answerin' the question."

"I think that's incredible," Dupree said.

"Me too. I was thunderstruck! I loved her more than ever."

"He loved me for my cows," Valericia said in a fake pout.

"Right. Anyway, we went to Argentina. Her folks weren't real happy with the news. But, I guess I grew on them because after the wedding her dad asked me to join the family business. It was an Aggie's dream come true. I tried, I really did, but after a couple of years I was so homesick I couldn't stand it."

"Then his father died," Valericia said sadly.

"The old man rolled a tractor on himself trying to cross a ditch. The wall crumbled, over she went. They say he died instantly, crushed to death. That was my excuse to come home. I really didn't think down deep she would come with me. On the airplane home, she told me she was expecting our daughter."

"My father never let me go if he knew," she said. "It was good we go."

"And here we are. El Rancho Grande." Chet chuckled at his joke. "The ranch went to her older brother so that probably wouldn't have worked out so well, in the end."

"That is a great story."

"Except the ending," Chet said.

"How's that?" Dupree frowned.

"Our daughter married a young man who works for the State. They live in Sacramento, so we see them often, but they have no interest in this old place. So when I go, four generations of Weaver's blood, sweat, and tears go with me."

"Do you have grandchildren?"

"Three," Valericia replied beaming with pride.

"Tucker, the oldest, love to come out here on holidays and in the summer and 'elp out. He says he wants to go to UC Davis just like Grandpa and Granma." Valericia's pride was showing.

"Well, there you go," Dupree offered.

"There I go where? He's just a high school kid," Chet said.

"He'll go to UC Davis, right?"

"That the plan," Valericia replied.

"From the looks of it, you, my friend, are far from dead."

"I can't leave it to him. The inheritance taxes alone would bury him. Besides, we can't leave his sisters anything to equal this place."

"You don't have to." Dupree was slipping into attorney mode. "You create a living trust. You make your grandson primary trustee, and give the girls an annual percentage of the farms net after, what's your grandson's name?"

"Tucker."

"After Tucker is paid a fair ranch manager's salary, the three of them split the net three ways. If he's good at his job, the girls get a nice check at the end of the year. If anything happens to Tucker, they split the sale of the place. Unless Tucker has a son, in which case the Weaver Ranch Trust goes to the son or sons with the same agreement. The pie just gets divided into more shares of the net."

"We can do such a thing?" Chet acted like the door to heaven just opened.

"Got a computer? A printer?"

"Yeah, in the office."

Dupree rose to his feet, a mug of tea in hand. "Let's go."

"What do you mean?" Chet asked.

"It's what I do."

Chet and Valericia stood and nearly ran from the room.

"One question!" Dupree called out at their backs.

The pair stopped and turned.

"What about your daughter?"

"She said at Thanksgiving, she wished there was a way Tucker could farm this place."

The office was a mess; papers, folders, and old Farm Journal magazines stacked everywhere. But on the desk was a brand-new computer.

"What? You think we were igger-unt clod busters?" Chet laughed. "Make yourself at home."

Dupree was completely in his element. His emotions were swelling as he put his fingers to the keyboard. His head throbbed, but the excitement of helping the Weavers helped him forget it for a while. Three hours, a roast beef sandwich, a Coke, and two more cups of tea later, Dupree finished The Chester and Valericia Weaver Family Trust.

Thanks to a clever IT guy in his office, Dupree's life was stored in The Cloud complete with unbreakable, untraceable, password and access. Not a soul would ever know he downloaded an unbreakable, iron-clad Trust template, both State and Federal Homestead exemptions, Pioneer Founders Status, and escrow protection instructions to protect generations of Weavers and their descendants from lawsuits challenging the document.

"All done," Dupree said with a big black-eyed smile. "I've marked all the places that need your signatures. They must be notarized. Your bank will probably do it for free." He held up three envelopes. "These must be mailed as soon as possible. Keep this in the safest place you've got. Make sure your daughter and Tucker both know where it is. Do you have a family attorney?"

"Yes," Valericia answered.

"Better yet, have them store it in their office with..." Dupree turned back to the computer, and moments later the printer chugged out another sheet of paper. "Sign this and give it to them. It is instructions for what to do in case of your passing."

"I don't know what to say," Chet began. "What do we owe you?"

"You can't afford me." Dupree laughed. "Just promise me the next poor guy that comes to you with a broken nose..." Dupree paused. "No, forget that part!"

Valericia bent and gave Dupree a gentle kiss on the cheek. "You are a good man. Please don't ever hurt yourself."

"I don't think that will ever happen," Dupree said solemnly.

"Thank you, God." Valericia crossed herself.

"You haven't told us what your plan is," Chet said.

"I heard about a little place called White Owl, Washington. That's where I was heading. So I guess I'll be back at it."

"I think not. Your days of hitchhiking ended today."

"That's right," Valericia agreed.

"Tomorrow we will take you to the train and buy you a ticket to get you as close to White Owl as possible, and a bus transfer to get you the rest of the way. It is the least we can do for your generosity." Chet nodded hard. "And no arguments. We have a spare room you are welcome to and a hot shower. Oh, and that bloody shirt has got to go. I got a closet full of birthday and Christmas shirts, and you are welcome to all you want."

"I accept. Two will do, it seems a fair trade, for services rendered."

"Not hardly, but it is a deal!" Chet thrust out his hand and Dupree shook it firmly.

As he stepped into the bathroom, he caught his reflection in the mirror over the sink. What he saw shocked him. Both his eyes were black and swollen. His nose was a small eggplant in the middle of his face. The stubble of three days' growth of beard did nothing to help the frightening face in front of him. Dupree ran his hands through his hair.

"You are in no condition for polite society." He turned from the mirror to the shower door.

Hot water sprayed hard on Dupree's neck and down his back. He rotated his head and tried to loosen his tight muscles. Washing felt good and long overdue. A melody came to his mind. He began to hum softly, then louder. Words came to the tune, and he sang them. Within moments he forgot where he was and with eyes closed, he was singing *Tramps like us, baby we were born to run*! at the top of his voice.

Dupree dressed in a yellow plaid shirt with pearl buttons he selected from Chet's closet. When he went into the kitchen, Valericia was holding out big mugs of steaming coffee.

"Morning Mr. Springsteen, did you rest well?"

"You heard me?"

"They heard you in Sacramento!" Chet teased.

"Stop, it was nice," Valericia chided.

"Thank you." Dupree bowed slightly.

In his past life, a remark about his shower singing would have angered and embarrassed Dupree and set the tone for the whole day. Somehow on this morning, with these people, it was just a natural part of the love and companionship of this house.

"I called the station; there is a train at eleven-thirty heading north. They never heard of White Owl, so I Googled it. You picked a dilly. You ever been there?"

"No, why?" Dupree's voice gave away his apprehension.

"As far as I can tell, it is about as far from Lawyerville as is humanly possible." Chet chuckled. "You like tie-dye, Zen Gatherings, and Americana Music Festivals?"

"I'm not sure. But if it is the opposite of high stress, twelve hundred dollar an hour, never satisfied clients, and wives with more social commitments than marital, and snotty kids with their hand out for money one minute, and their tongue sticking out at you the next, I'm in!"

"Good, 'cause you got a ticket, and the train leaves in three hours," Chet confirmed.

"I hope you are hungry," Valericia said, as she slid a plate of eggs, bacon, potatoes, and toast in front of Dupree.

"Starving." He smiled up at her.

After breakfast, Chet took Dupree on a tour of the ranch in his Jeep. Most of the land was fallow. Chet explained that he just couldn't afford to pay all the taxes on the ever-increasing payroll to harvest row crops. A large portion of the land in the back was irrigated and lush green. A herd of red and white cattle grazed near a large pond.

"Purebred Hereford stock. Never been crossbred since my great-granddad's time. We raise them purely for breeding purposes. There is a large return to heritage lines. It all started with tomatoes, of all things. People want food like it was a hundred years ago. I never imagined my father and grandfather's absolutely fanatical dedication to keeping the line pure would pay off one day. I wish they could see the market now. They'd never believe it. I get as much for a bull as they used to get for a herd."

"Have you registered the DNA? Big money there. You need to look into it. It's kind of like a patent. If those cows are as pure as you say. It could be worth a lot more than you think. Call your alma mater, ask them. Then get a good lawyer."

"I thought you were my lawyer."

"I'm retired," Dupree said with a smile.

"Couldn't prove it by me!"

"You need an Agricultural attorney; UC Davis can probably help with that too."

"Look at the time! We gotta get you to the train!" Chet whirled the Jeep around and started back to the house. "You get me going on those cows and I can talk all day."

"That's why you were born to do this. I can see your passion. It's a wonderful thing, Chet. I envy you."

"You'll get yours back. Maybe not in L.A., but you were on fire last night. You got it, you're just looking for a new outlet. Trust me, the time will come."

Back at the house, Valericia was waiting on the porch. As the Jeep pulled up next to the house, she slapped her forehead in mock exasperation.

"I know, I know!" Chet pleaded.

"Rojas Vacas!"

"You grab your stuff and I'll get the car," Chet called back as he ran toward the garage.

In the spare room, Dupree smiled down at his bloody thrift store shirt in the wastepaper basket, as he carefully rolled his new shirt and stuffed it in his pack. Minutes later, the Weavers and Dupree were in the car and flying down the freeway toward the train station.

It was a strange parting for Dupree. He was a person of frequent and shallow encounters and acquaintances. His social circle was suspect at best, his colleagues were just that, and his family was a disaster. Somehow, in just a few hours he formed a bond with a couple of total strangers that pained his heart to part from.

"I've got to say this has been one incredible meeting. Your generosity is a treasure we will cherish. That paperwork you did, my goodness sakes, that's something we would never have dreamed of. And the DNA of the cattle thing, I just don't have words."

"All in a day's work." Dupree smiled.

"Don't take it lightly. You just changed lives here, my friend." Emotion overtook Chet and he couldn't speak. He turned and walked to the ticket counter.

"And I'm the one with brain damage," Valericia stammered. "You promise to come see us again?"

"I certainly will try. Thank you so much for patching me up."

"You look like I beat you up!" Valericia laughed.

From off in the distance, a long wail of a train whistle announced it was approaching the station.

"Just in time," Chet said, thrusting out the ticket envelope.

The train roared into the station, drowning whatever Valericia tried to say. Dupree looked at the smiling couple and felt the Trust he did for them was of more value than all the corporate law, legal maneuvering, or intimidating letters he ever wrote. He felt a sense of pride in the service, not in the victory or deal-making, but in the ability of his knowledge to actually do good in someone's life. Dupree thought of Tucker, the high school kid that would go to UC Davis, become an Aggie, and then securely be the fifth generation to raise cattle on his family's land, and he smiled.

After a bit of small talk and waiting, came the "All aboard." Dupree hugged Valericia, and a handshake turned into a manly bear hug for Chet as well. As he boarded the train, Dupree turned to see them standing hand in hand, waving. He gave them a big smile, and to his utter amazement, blew them a kiss.

Chapter 7

The train rolled along and Dupree self-consciously looked out the window. Women who passed him seemed to hold their bags a little tighter. One little girl asked her mother loudly, "Mommy, what's wrong with that man?" It was at that point Dupree decided to face the window. The landscape changed little in the first hour, but gradually it began to incline and the grass greened.

Trees, oaks at first then pines, began to appear. There was a peace that overcame Dupree. This time he would have no contact with the driver. There was no waiting except with his new friends on the platform at the station. He felt a little foolish not thinking of the anonymity of train travel sooner. His thoughts were soon shattered.

"Mind if I sit here?"

"No," Dupree said, turning to face the young man slipping into the seat across the table.

"Damn, what's the other guy look like?"

"Like the one with the gun."

"Pistol whipped?"

"That's what they call it."

"I'm Foster," the man said, as he wriggled across the seats to adjust his weight next to the window.

"Dupree."

"How far you goin'?"

"Washington."

"Portland for me." Foster grinned, exposing a chipped front tooth.

Dupree took in his new acquaintance. He guessed late teens, early twenties, but he could be even younger. Dupree wasn't good at judging age, so he tried to use his son as a measure. The shirt he wore was freshly pressed but the hours on the train left deep creases where he leaned and crossed his thin pale arms.

"I love trains, don't you? I mean, what is more American than hopping on the Iron Horse and riding into the wind?"

"Foster, you are quite the poet."

"Lonely headlight on a northbound train, brings cattle and timber, but takes my love, and leaves me in pain." Foster sang in a clear engaging tenor. "That's what I do. I'm a folksinger, country singer, like from years past. None of this straw hat, fake hole in your jeans, Hawaiian shirt crap they call country today. I'm more the Western half of Country Western."

"I'm no judge of music, but I liked it. Is that what you're going to do in Portland?"

"I've got a gig playin' with a band called Weeds and Wire. They call their stuff Americana. I don't care what they call it as long as I can sing my songs. I got a guitar case full. No guitar," Foster grinned. "I'll get a new one when I get there. The songs are more important. 'Sides, I don't have a suitcase, so my clothes are in there too."

"How old are you, Foster?" Dupree asked.

"Oh, don't you start. Twenty-three. I know, I know, what's a kid know about trains, broken hearts, and hard travelin'." Foster's grin was gone and the face of an artist's defiance glared across the table.

"Quite the contrary, I was wondering how someone so young had such an old soul."

"I'm kind of a story magnet. I like to sit and listen to the old folks' talk of when they were young. They're all dyin' off you know? So somebody needs to capture their light and put it in song. I figured it might as well be me. I was never good at school. I really didn't fit in with the kids my age, they never listen. They only care about cell phones, Snaptwits, ChatFace, and those big-ass sisters on the cover of every magazine 'tween here and hell. I cut all that loose when I turned seventeen. I been on the road since. Usually, I'm ridin' in the boxcars, not up front with the ticketed folks."

Dupree chuckled. "When I was in college I listened to this guy for a while that told people he ran away from home at ten, twelve, thirteen, fifteen, fifteen and a half, seventeen and eighteen, was born in New Mexico, worked in a carnival singing his songs, and rode the rails with hobos.

"Turned out he was from an upper-middle-class Jewish family in Minnesota, and never ran anywhere. He did travel to New York to meet his idol, Woody Guthrie, when he was twenty though. That changed the face of music forever. He won a Nobel Prize for Literature, too. His name's Bob Dylan. Ever hear of him?"

"Yes, sir," Foster said sheepishly.

"Want to start over?"

"My name is Peter James. I'm from Merced. My dad's a high school English teacher. My mom's just a mom. I went to Golden Valley High School, where my dad taught, and I spent two years at Merced Junior College. Happy?"

"Are you? You know, being one's self is far more important than creating an image that you think will sell. I'm learning that pretty late. I bet you sat here because of the black eyes. Right?"

"So how'd you really get them?"

"I got pistol-whipped while hitchhiking. Aren't you listening? The truth is far more interesting than some borrowed persona of what you think you should be."

"I really am going to Portland to play in a band."

"I'm sure you are."

"They saw my YouTube video and liked my song. I did more, and they like them too."

"Now, that is much more interesting and impressive than the whole *Bound for Glory* nonsense."

"What's that?"

"It's a book by Woody Guthrie. Your dad teaches English and you never heard of *Bound for Glory*?"

"It's not his fault, the school..."

"It never is," Dupree interrupted.

Peter "Foster" James sat quietly looking out the window.

Bound for Glory, Dupree thought. Where in the world did that come from? He read it as a junior in high school. He was trying to make points with a girl in his history class that always carried around a beat-up guitar. Vicki Templeman, nouveau-hippie, child of communist parents who were the scourge of their homeowner's association, head of every committee and petition in town his father was against and didn't celebrate the holidays of organized religion or the bourgeois misinformation media. Dupree was totally in love with her for about three months, until Jennifer Wenerholtzer, a Dutch exchange student, transferred into his English class.

"What'd you mean, it never is?"

"How long has he been teaching?"

"I guess about twenty-five years."

"Does he belong to the union?"

"Sure, and they almost went on strike a couple of years ago," Peter said excitedly.

"Then they can't fire him. He has tenure, near retirement, the union would never allow it, they would defend his 'Academic Freedom.' He could teach any book he wanted. If he wanted. My bet is he is burned out, hates kids, the administration, and can't wait to retire."

"What makes you think you're so smart?"

"I'm not, but if you intend to tell the truth, capture the light, like you were saying, you have to be able to see the truth no matter how much it hurts, or inconvenient to the narrative you have written for yourself."

"My dad's a good teacher."

"I'm sure he is. But we all, sooner or later, see the futility in what we're doing. When it becomes 'not our fault' we have resigned our authority to someone else. Then it's time to get out. Do something else. Become Foster, so to speak. The real truth to your 'Foster story' is that you didn't fit in. That's the artist trying to break free. It's not my fault I don't have any friends. That's when you gave in to the bullies, cool kids and jocks. You did great YouTube videos, right?"

"Yeah."

"I bet you have never played in front of an audience in your life." Dupree smiled at the scowling kid in front of him. "Have you?"

"No, but..."

"No buts, where's your guitar?" Dupree pressed.

"Back in the carry-on rack."

"Go get it."

"What?"

"You heard me, go get it."

The young man scooted out of the seat and up the aisle, past the senior citizens, Mexican families, and hipsters with the silly little hats, big beards, backpacks, and earbuds. A couple of minutes later Peter returned with a guitar case that never left his bedroom, until today.

"Nice case. Open it up." Dupree insisted.

"Why?"

"You'll see."

Peter obeyed and took out a shiny Taylor guitar that obviously never saw a minute of hard traveling.

Dupree stood to his feet and at the top of his voice said to the hundred or so people in the train car, "Ladies and Gentleman, Senors y Senoras, it is my honor and privilege to introduce an incredible new talent on the train with us today, Foster James!" Dupree began to applaud and so did the captive audience on the train.

"I can't..." the young man said, quaking in fear.

"Then you never will," Dupree replied, then sat down.

Foster James stood, put the guitar strap around his neck and cleared his throat. "I would like to…" he said strumming his guitar nervously, "I would like to sing you a song called He Held My Hand."

The first verse was shaky and slightly ahead of the guitar, but the chorus rang out bright, clear, and confident. That moment Foster James, singer-songwriter and newest member of Weeds and Wire, was born.

Three songs later, and after enthusiastic applause, he sat down.

"How'd that feel?" Dupree grinned.

"Oh my God, oh my God, it was like pure energy shining out from every pore of my body. They liked my songs. What a feeling, what a, I don't know, moment. I never want to lose it. Ever." The young singer was barely able to contain his delight.

"I hope you never do," Dupree nodded.

Foster began patting his pockets and finally found what he was looking for. "Want a Snickers? I mean to celebrate, I mean, to say thank you."

"I didn't do anything, you wrote the songs."

"Yeah, but you made me sing them."

"I just nudged. Yeah, give me half of that." Dupree laughed.

The sugary candy bar was not what the kid needed. A few minutes later he shook hands with Dupree and went to the next car.

Well after dark, Foster returned.

"Well, hello," Dupree said when Foster tapped his shoulder.

"I sang in every car behind us! Look at this!" He reached in his pocket and pulled out a wad of bills and a handful of change. "Can life get any better? I was just heading for the cars that way. Thanks again."

"Good luck in Portland," Dupree offered, but Foster was already heading up the aisle to the next car.

The lights dimmed in the rail car and the conductor approached Dupree. "Would you like a pillow or blanket or anything? It gets a bit chilly though the mountains."

"Yes, that would be great. Leaning on this window is kind of rough on my head."

"The seat does lay back."

"I know, but it makes my nose throb. I tried it earlier."

"You get in a wreck?"

"No, long story."

"I got all night," the conductor said skeptically.

"I got pistol-whipped and dumped while hitchhiking."

"Okay, I get it, none of my business. Have a good night." The conductor handed Dupree a pillow in a plastic bag and a blanket to match.

"No, really that's what happened."

"Uh-huh," the conductor replied in disbelief, as he turned to the next passenger.

Dupree unwrapped the blanket and pillow and placed the plastic wrappers on the table. He wound the strap of his pack around his arm and covered up with the blanket. It took a little adjusting, but he found just the spot between his head and the glass for the pillow, closed his eyes, and as the train rattled along through the night, he fell fast asleep.

Perhaps it was the rocking of the rail car, perhaps it was the relative safety of his environment or the occasional dull throbbing of his nose, but Dupree began to dream. Dupree was not given to dreaming. The stress and Rubik's Cube puzzles of the law usually just kept him awake. He would pace, self-medicate with a double Scotch, or simply toss and turn, but dreams rarely visited his four or five hours of sleep a night.

Tonight he slid and floated through a world of images, fleeting vignettes, tableaux, and disjointed memories. All were meaningless, and yet profound. None were worrisome or unpleasant. It all started from a place of discomfort but ended in a place of tranquility. At one point he was sitting at his desk at the firm. In the corner, Ray Charles sat a grand piano singing Born to Lose, as Dupree tried to assemble a model airplane. Just an image, one of the hundreds, then it was gone.

The longest of his dreams seemed to go on and on, though probably it was only a few seconds. He was riding a bicycle through his childhood neighborhood. The houses, cars, and people he saw were familiar but somehow sad and forlorn.

Mr. Bonaventure flagged him down. The old man, who every year hand-delivered Easter Baskets and Christmas candy canes to the neighborhood children, spoke to him with disappointment and discernible anger.

"Why you never come back to the neighborhood?" The old man's thick Italian accent was still the same. "You left to go to college and I not see you again. You let me die without a good-bye. I thought you liked me? What happened to you in that college?"

"I..." Dupree began, but the old man turned and walked away.

He rode on, and one old neighbor after another turned their backs when they saw him. Finally, he reached his house. His bike came to a stop on the grass and he let it fall.

"I'm home," he called as he opened the door.

There didn't seem to be anyone home. The sights and smells of his childhood home were the same, but there were pictures of movie stars in the picture frames on the walls and mantle. Dupree walked toward the kitchen. Suddenly he saw his parents in the shadows. As he approached he saw that they were old, much older than they ever lived to be. As they backed into the light of the kitchen, he could see they were hunched and twisted with age. His mother looked up at Dupree, but the face so wrinkled and old, it was not his mother at all, but his wife, Diane. She sneered and snapped, "It's about time you got back, where have you been?" His father turned to her and shook his head.

"I never liked you. You are a mean nasty woman who made my boy mean and unhappy. Why don't you ever die?"

"I am dead you fool, just watch!"

The old woman began to twirl in the middle of the kitchen. Her skirt rose as she spun and exposed a pair of young slender legs and sparkling silver tennis shorts. Dupree laughed loudly and began moving to his father. He put his arm around his frail old shoulders and they both laughed as the twirling sped up. Faster and faster she spun until she lifted off the floor and up through a hole that appeared in the ceiling.

"We could have had a lot of fun, son. Why were you so ashamed of me?"

"Would you like to go on a bike ride with me?" Dupree offered in return.

"Sure!" his father cheerfully responded. When Dupree looked at him, he was a young man again.

In an instant they were pedaling down the street, merrily waving and greeting all the neighbors. As they pedaled, Dupree was watching himself on the bike. He was no longer a participant, but an observer. As he watched, he and his father faded into the green arch at the end of the old street.

If he could have seen himself, Dupree would have seen a man smiling in his sleep, bobbing his head to the music of his dreams.

The blood-curdling scream of a baby jerked Dupree from his sleep. The Mexican woman, her family still sleeping, paced the aisle. She gave Dupree an apologetic grimace. He smiled in return and tried to go back to sleep. The purple of dawn was filling the sky and he just leaned against the window. He tried to recall some of the best parts of his dreams, but they were like a mist burning away in the dawning of the day. A warmth of spirit came over him as if he was released of guilt and anger, pain, and exhaustion. The gentle movement of the train brought a smile to his face and the screaming baby was just so much noise, blending with the roar of the train in the coming light.

The station clock out the window said six twenty as the train came to a stop in Ashland. Somewhere in the night, they crossed the border into Oregon. The platform was crowded with suitcases, boxes reinforced with twine, and an army of passengers they belonged to, and their family and friends.

The hipsters in his car stood and made a great production of stretching, running their hands through odd cuts of hair thick with gel. One of the big bearded leaders of the oh, so cool band of travelers reached down and lifted his waifish girlfriend from her seat and spun her in the aisle nearly, hitting an elderly lady with a walker. He set his curly blond partner aside and offered the old woman a spin but she declined. With a tip of his hat and a deep bow, he waved her on.

The Mexican family gathered up the children, bundles, diaper bags, and plastic bags of food and made their way out of the car. Within minutes nearly half of the familiar faces were gone.

A tired mechanical voice came through the overdriven speakers. "Ashland station. We will have a twenty-minute stop. Please take your belongings if you leave the train, we can't be responsible for any missing or lost items. Ashland station twenty-minute stop."

Dupree decided to stretch his legs. He opened the magazine he found on the table, placed the sack lunch Valericia sent with him in the seat and set his coffee cup from the vending machine next to the magazine.

"That looks occupied," he said, leaving his seat.

"I'll keep an eye on it for you," the lady across the aisle offered.

"Thank you. I've grown fond of this seat."

"I know what you mean." The woman smiled.

On the platform, Dupree made his way through the crowd and into the station. With his pack securely across his chest, he made his way to the bathroom. The lobby of the station was nearly empty, except for a couple of people still purchasing tickets.

As Dupree pushed the restroom door open with his forearm, he heard a loud harsh voice coming from inside. The profanity that filled the air seemed to be aimed at no one and everyone. As the oaths and blasphemies echoed against the tile and porcelain, Dupree identified the direction of the tirade. He moved slowly around the divider separating the sinks and urinals from the stalls.

Near the end of the row of stalls protruded a leg from under the door. The foot was twisted in a most unnatural position. It wagged back and forth banging against the frame of the stall. Twice it disappeared under door only to shoot back out a different limb, followed by a deep groan and another string of curses.

Carefully assessing the situation, Dupree surmised the person in the stall was unable to get up.

"Having trouble?"

"No, you dumb shit, I'm having a party in here. Yes, I'm having trouble!"

"Can I give you a hand?" Dupree replied in a calm civil tone.

"Yes, please." The voice inside the stall mellowed a bit. "Please, yes, I need help."

"Help is on the way," Dupree answered in a friendly, yet cautious, voice.

Grabbing the handle of the stall Dupree was presented with his first problem in his Good Samaritan effort. The door was locked.

The voice inside the stall stated he locked the door before he fell, then called it an astounding variety of names and cursed it to unspeakable tortures of hell.

"I get you're upset but can you dial back your language just a bit? I'll try and figure out how to get the door open." Dupree, not unfamiliar with his own burning blast of profanity on occasion, found the man inside the stall beyond the bounds of even bad taste.

"Whatever," the man groaned.

Dupree glanced around the restroom for some kind of tool, then walked back to look around the divider.

"Hey, where you goin'? Don't leave me in here!" the man yelled.

"Relax, I'm looking for something to help me get the door open."

"Well for God's sake, don't go gathering a crowd."

Dupree didn't respond. Just around the corner, leaning next to the urinals, was a mop and heavy industrial bucket. He commandeered the rolling opportunity. The uneven clattering of the rollers on the tile echoed off the walls. He pushed the flat side of the bucket with the ringer against the door. Getting a tight grasp on the top of the door frame, Dupree placed one foot and then the other on the edge of the heavy yellow bucket.

Dupree took a breath and looked over the top of the door, not sure what he would find. Wedged between the wall and the unflushed toilet was a young man with a military haircut. His legs were sprawled in front of him and a pair of metal canes were lodged behind his back.

His face and neck showed the scars of severe burns. Next to the toilet on the other side set a tan camouflage bag. He was undoubtedly a wounded warrior.

"Good morning," Dupree said, his head appearing over the door.

The young man didn't answer, just looked down at his legs. "Damn things don't work right or something. They both buckled back at the same time. I can't get up. Three people so far have just ignored me. What kind of asshole leaves a person in a state like this?"

"We got this. We'll have you out of here and on your way in a minute." Dupree reassured him. "I can't tell, does that latch go up and to the right or left?"

"My left, your right."

"Okay, hang on." Dupree reached down and grabbed the mop handle, thankfully it was dry and the bucket was empty. He swung the business end of the mop up and over the top of the stall.

It took three tries but the mop strings finally caught in the knob on the latch and up it came.

"You did it! Hot damn! Good goin'."

Dupree put one foot on the floor and the bucket shot out from under him and slammed against the bathroom wall, the mop flopping to the floor.

"Alright, how are we going to get you up and out of here?" Dupree asked, surveying the situation.

"I think if you can get me under the arms to give me some stability, I can help lift until I get these pieces of shit straightened out."

"Let's give it a try."

Dupree bent and put his arms under the young man's and lifted firmly, but gently. He could hear and feel the metal legs click and turn into place.

"Hey, I think we got it. Can you grab the canes?"

As the young man balanced with one hand on the wall of the stall, Dupree retrieved the four-footed canes.

"Other than your wounded pride, are you hurt anywhere? Your back okay?"

"My ass is asleep, but otherwise I'm okay, I guess."

Dupree stepped back and out of the way. With surprising agility, the young man made his way out of the stall.

"I am very grateful, sir. Thank you for getting me out of there."

"How long have you been stuck in there?" Dupree asked.

"Since about three-thirty, I reckon."

"My name's Dupree. Sorry it took so long to get you out of there."

"First Gunnery Sergeant Devon McAllister, in your debt sir." McAllister offered his hand to Dupree.

"No, I'm in your debt. Thank you for your sacrifice and service to our nation." Dupree patted the Marine on the shoulder, then shook his hand firmly. "Got time for a cup of coffee?"

"I'd like that."

Dupree let McAllister take the lead. Halfway to the door, Dupree stopped.

"Hold on, I came in here for another reason than getting you unstuck!" Dupree laughed and walked to the urinal.

"I've had enough of this place. I'll wait outside."

When Dupree left the restroom, McAllister was sitting on a bench making adjustments to his prosthetics.

"Black, cream, sugar?" Dupree asked.

"Black, thanks."

The coffee was horrible. The thin paper cups were only three-quarters full, but the Marine was happy to get it.

"So, where are you headed?" Dupree asked once seated.

"Longbridge, Texas."

"I should have known you were a Texan."

"The mouth?" McAllister chuckled. "Nope, that's pure United States Marine Corp. I gotta clean that up. My pop's a Baptist preacher and it won't sit well at all with him, or my mom. God knows I know better. And you?"

"I'm going to take a look at a little town called White Owl, Washington. I'd like to see if I can find a place to catch my breath and maybe start over." Dupree felt at ease with Devon McAllister and wasn't hesitant to share what he was thinking.

"Northbound 318, will be leaving in five minutes," the loudspeaker announced.

"You need help getting rescheduled? I got a couple of minutes."

"No, I'm good, thanks. If your trip to White Owl doesn't pan out, come on down to Texas for a while. You get to Longbridge, ask anybody for Pastor Jack's house, and you got a home."

"That is an offer that has the sound of real promise."

"And the best biscuits and gravy in the Lone Star State!"

"I suppose if you've got it from here, I should get back to my train." Dupree extended his hand. "Nice to meet you, Devon, maybe next time it won't be so stressful."

"Yes sir, next time it will be BBQ and potato salad and ice tea."

"You'll have me switching tickets in a minute!" Dupree stood and gave Devon a nod and walked to the exit.

Dupree hated war. He hated waste. He despised the waste of young men and women's lives. He hated the waste of twisted scarred bodies that would ache, and long to be whole, for the rest of their lives.

The wars in Iraq and Afghanistan continued year after year. America tired of the news, the pictures, and reports. Other tragedies, scandals, and catastrophes grabbed the headlines. Politicians posed and postured and did nothing. The nation grew numb to the pain and suffering of the women and children trapped in a hellish cycle of bombings, and village to village taking and retaking of land. Refugee camps and the mass exodus to Europe, the hatred and hostility of the people of the overrun countries and their cultures, by people who neither wanted to assimilate or embrace their new country of residence, ushered in a whole new set of problems, wasted resources, and lives.

What angered Dupree, apart from the loss of American lives, injuries, and shattered lives of the Veterans, was the waste of money. Trillions and trillions of dollars wasted on people who hated each other for millennia, who shared a common religion but hated the sects of their countrymen. Americans fight and die for people who, left to their own devices, would still be fighting and killing each other in another thousand years.

There was no gratitude, benefit, or significant change in lands of rock and sand. Yet every night on the evening news, people are asked to give money to feed Native Americans in Arizona and South Dakota. Funds are sought hourly for families, and veterans, ripped apart by these pointless political wars. With all his knowledge of the law and the structure of government, there was nothing Dupree could do to affect change anywhere. And that, to him, was the greatest waste of all, and he hated it.

Voting was pointless, so he stopped twenty years ago. The political parties were both the same when it came right down to it. Liberal, Conservative were simply two names for the same dog. The only real difference in the legislation they passed, in the end, was where the money was spent. The pot was divided quietly, in bills that had more provisions and amendments than anyone could possibly define, trace, or fully understand. Elected officials either stayed in Washington and got rich, or left and got richer. So Dupree tried not to focus on the news and the decline in western civilization. It would continue to decay until it all collapsed under its own greedy, bloated, immoral weight, and he would be dead and buried by then.

At the door, Dupree turned and gave a last look at the warrior who suffered the humiliation of being trapped for three hours on the filthy floor of a train station restroom in the country he gave his legs for. Dupree shed an angry tear, turned, and ran to the train.

For a moment he thought he boarded the wrong car. He scoured the car for a familiar face. The turnover at the Ashland station was considerable. He moved up the aisle and got curious looks from strangers. It was then he remembered his broken nose and black eyes.

Not once in their time together did Devon McAllister react or question his injuries. Not once did he catch him staring at the bandages or deep purple circles around his eyes. Could it be he was so used to broken bodies and bruises he didn't notice? Dupree smiled. He suddenly didn't feel self-conscious about his wounds. He would wear them in Devon's honor. Then he spotted the woman who promised to keep his seat.

At his seat, his belongings sat undisturbed, but across from them sat a woman reading a book.

Chapter 8

"Hello," Dupree said in greeting.

The woman neither looked up nor responded. Dupree took his seat. He took his pack off his shoulder and placed it between him and the wall. He closed the magazine and put the empty coffee cup in the plastic bag on the hook under the window.

The woman looked over the top of her paperback and sneered. Dupree smiled. She huffed and went back to her book.

"Thank you for saving my seat," Dupree said to the woman across the aisle.

"Oh, no problem." She smiled and paused. "Does that hurt as bad as it looks?"

"Only when somebody mentions it." Dupree chuckled.

"Oops, sorry."

"How far are you going?"

"Oh, just to Salem. Visiting my kids for a few days."

"Nice." Dupree nodded.

"You?"

"I'm headed for a little town in Washington, up in the mountains. How about you?" Dupree asked, turning to the woman seated across the table.

"How about me what?"

"Where are you heading to?"

"If you must know, Portland for work, Scorpio, Republican, O Positive, and not interested."

"In what?" Dupree asked.

"In continuing this pointless conversation."

Dupree studied the woman for a long moment. He took in her Versace, single men find you unapproachable or so you claim, though you would kill for a boyfriend, demeanor.

"Top of your class in law school, Magna cum laude at some state college somewhere, thus the need to overachieve to compensate. The thing I don't quite get is why you're on this train. Afraid of flying, lost your license due to a third DUI? No, you'd have been fired. I got it, inner ear problems from eating too many aspirins for headaches putting in the hours you think will make you partner." Dupree smiled at the woman. "How'd I do?"

"Gucci briefcase, twelve hundred. I try to relax before big meetings by reading. Usually, I can get all the way to Salem without being accosted by some broke down lady's man, not to mention carnival trick, smart asses."

Dupree laughed and did a drum roll on the table with the tips of his fingers. "So, who do you work for, if it isn't a source of embarrassment?"

"You are?" she paused.

"Just the firm please."

"Johnson, Poulsen and Raye."

"Never heard of them. Land use litigation?" Dupree asked.

"I'm not talking to you."

"It is a dead-end. You got too much going for you to get stuck in Backwater, Oregon, shuttling papers back and forth to the Capitol. That's why you're on the train. They're too cheap to pay mileage, and your aging Toyota can't stand up to miles."

"Just who are you?"

"Name's Dupree."

"Never heard of you."

"In your circles, I imagine not. I have hired, and not, a thousand just like you. It's show biz kid, you have to hit the big note, get the big laugh, or ring the last tear out of your big scene. You have thirty seconds to do it in the big leagues.

"Problem is, there is nowhere in this entire state for you to show your chops to anyone who makes a difference. You got spunk and style. Go to L.A. or New York, short of that, Chicago. I'd have hired you."

"For a black-eyed yahoo on a train from Ashland, you got a pretty good act, but I'll wait for the movie." She grabbed her briefcase and book and left the table.

"Bitch," said the woman across the aisle.

"No, no, she is a very powerful young woman who is just too full of herself at the moment for her ears to work." Dupree watched her stomp up the aisle. "Give her another five years. She'll wake up."

"Where'd you get all that? Is it a trick, like on TV?"

"Years of working in a world filled with people just like her. Some rise to the top, but most burn out, change professions, or become single person offices that sue for damages, collect on court awards, write up wills, and negotiate leases in strip malls."

Out the window, the sky was filling with threatening gray clouds. Before Dupree could fully appreciate the change in the weather, the clouds opened and a torrential rain drenched the countryside. The rain was a welcome distraction from the sunshine and dry grass of the mile upon mile of California freeways. The emerald fields of alfalfa, and plants Dupree could not identify, were pleasing to the eye and calming to the spirit. Small towns, and even smaller wide spots in the road rolled by, punctuated by old barns and even older houses. Cars at crossings watched and occasionally waved as the train flew past.

Dupree stretched his legs out and rested them on the seat across from him. The car was quiet and there was very little movement, soon his eyes grew heavy. He let them rest, and before long he fell asleep. The jerking of the train braking woke him. As Dupree opened his eyes, he was greeted by a big blue and white Medford station sign.

Nearly half the car exited when the train came to a stop. Out the window, the platform was crowded with dreadlocks, tie-dye, madras skirts, and huge backpacks. Everywhere he looked were green, yellow, and black striped knit caps, Grateful Dead t-shirts, alpaca print ponchos, and marijuana leaf patches.

In the midst of the hippie gathering of the tribes stood a middle-aged Asian couple. Each held a small travel bag and laptop computer case. They smiled uncomfortably and waited patiently to board the train. Dupree hoped against hope that he would be able to have them sit with him. The thought of fifty or a hundred miles of patchouli oil, body odor, and wet hair was almost more than he could stand.

The conductor announced the "all aboard" and the crowd on the platform moved toward the doors. Oddly, there was nowhere near the number of people boarding as Dupree originally thought. The hemp and deadlock crowd moving toward the train was only a fraction of the passengers. Most were left behind waving and cheering from the platform.

The well-dressed Asian couple entered the far end of the car and began their way up the aisle. Dupree turned and looked out the window in hopes they wouldn't see his appearance and be put off at the thought of sitting with him. To his delight, he felt them place their bags on the table. He quickly put his feet down.

"May we join you?" the man asked.

"Please do," Dupree answered, still not turning fully.

The woman slid in first and her husband followed. They moved quickly, unpacking small laptop computers, two books and a larger volume that looked like a Bible, but in a light tan cover. Dupree slowly turned and faced them. They placed the tan book between them and each placed their books to their left.

"Going far?" the woman asked.

"Washington," Dupree replied.

"We are going to Vancouver, to see our new grandson." The woman smiled brightly and her eyes sparkled with excitement.

"Our first," the man nodded in agreement.

"That's wonderful," Dupree smiled. "Congratulations."

"Thank you." The woman offered her hand and said, "We are the Chens. I'm Jill and this is my husband, Michael."

Dupree shook her hand, then her husband's. "I'm Dupree. Nice to meet you, I was hoping you would join me. I was not excited at the prospect of a couple of those kids being with me for who knows how long."

"Oh, thank you very much."

"We like to ride the train. We can walk around, read and just relax."

"Looks like you are all set up there." Dupree indicated the books and computers.

"Yes, this works out well, they even have plugs!" Jill said, unwinding her power cord.

Dupree never noticed, but there was an electrical plug at the end of the table.

"Are you teachers?"

"Goodness, no! This is our Bible study."

"Looked like something academic."

"We find it very challenging at times. Study takes a lot of time, thought and prayer," Michael said.

"Where are you folks from. Medford?" Dupree asked.

"You mean where did we get these accents?" Jill giggled.

"No, I..."

"It's OK, I was teasing. We are originally from Taiwan. Now we live in Washington, D.C. We're retired."

"Nice. What kind of work did you do?"

"Internet Technology for the government, I worked for the Federal Reserve."

"I worked for the Treasury Department," Michael chimed in.

"You certainly don't look old enough to be retired." Dupree smiled.

"We came to the U.S. thirty-seven years ago. We've been married forty years," Jill proclaimed proudly. "I think it's time."

"Wonderful. Not many people make it that many years. I didn't."

"When there are three partners in a marriage it is easy."

"Excuse me?" Dupree was shocked by this delightful little woman's response.

"Jesus, Michael, and I make a perfect team."

"I see." Dupree didn't want the whole you need Jesus spiel.

"Oh, sorry. Never talk about religion or politics with strangers."

"Usually works best," Dupree agreed.

"Can we have our lunch yet?" Michael asked, breaking the tension.

Jill picked up one of the travel bags between them. "It's only eight o'clock! He's always hungry."

She pulled two plastic containers from the bag. Michael took one and removed the lid. Grapes. Jill popped another lid. That container was stuff with sliced red and yellow bell peppers.

"Something's missing," Michael complained.

"Hold on, I've got it." Jill reached into the bag and pulled out a small bundle of something wrapped in aluminum foil.

"You must try one of these. Jill makes the best egg rolls in the world." The foil was pulled back to reveal a couple of dozen dark brown crispy egg rolls. "I hope you're not Jewish or vegan because she loads them up with spicy ginger pork. Try one."

"Sounds great." Dupree took an egg roll. He didn't realize he was so hungry. "Wow! That is the best egg roll I've ever tasted."

"Didn't I tell you?" Michael beamed.

"Absolutely delicious. Jill, you win the blue ribbon."

Dupree savored every bite. What a nice couple, he thought. If they leave off the Jesus stuff we'll get along just fine. Still chewing, he turned to look out the window.

The rain poured and the train rolled on. What a nice way to spend a day, Dupree thought. Safe, warm, and great scenery. His mind drifted to a summer his family went to Yellowstone National Park. It was one of the few real vacations they ever took. His father nervously plotted out each day, mileage and distance to the next destination. His mother made sandwiches and divided potato chips on the tailgate of their Chevy Impala station wagon. The sights and sounds of that trip still bring a smile to his face. That trip he heard his father sing for the first and last time in his life. For no apparent reason, other than a spontaneous outburst of sheer joy, his parents sang all the verses and choruses of *Happy Trails to You*, complete with, what Dupree would later learn were, harmonies.

He smiled at the melancholy memory. It was a time he truly loved his family and the time they spent traveling the roads of western America. In an uncharacteristic change of plans, his father decided they would not go back the way they came but would travel on to see Mount Rushmore.

"Are you sure, Papa?" he remembered his mother questioning.

"My beautiful wife and wonderful son deserve the best trip this old shoe dog can give them!" His father slapped the steering wheel with his palm. "See the USA in a Chevrolet!" Again his father burst into song, with words of the TV commercial theme song. Dupree was dumbfounded. He and his mother laughed and then sang along as the ditty was repeated.

The back of the station wagon was transported into a magic carpet where Dupree would lay and watch the tall mountains and tree go by. Propped up by pillows and cushioned by blankets, it was his window on the world for those two weeks that summer.

His parents would sit close together on the big bench seat. Once or twice when the schedule required, his mother would drive and his father would nap, his head leaning against the window frame and the wind messing his normally perfect hair.

His mother would sing and hum songs from church. Once she even sang a lovely version of *Goodnight my Someone* from The Music Man. She often played the soundtrack of the Broadway musical when she dusted the house. It was her favorite record.

They took lots of pictures on the trip, and when they returned home his mother placed them all in an album with little notations and mementos she picked up on the trip.

That was the best time their family ever spent together. Dupree still kept that photo album, one of the few things of his parents he bothered with. A furrowed frown crossed his brow as he realized he would never see it again.

It was the last vacation they ever took. Upon their return, his father was informed that Danny, the assistant manager he left in charge of the store, stole the two weeks of receipts and disappeared the night before they got home. The District Manager informed his father that the loss would be adjusted against his annual sales that his yearly bonus was based on. That year there was no bonus. His father's paranoia and lack of self-confidence took a death blow to the midsection. From then on, he would never leave for more than a day or two. So their travels were limited to a trip to the lake or a quick day at the beach. Dupree never heard his father sing again, and he never saw him look at the photo album.

"Would you like another egg roll, Mr. Dupree?" Jill asked.

The packet of egg rolls was nearly gone. "Yes please, they're wonderful."

"Did you enjoy your nap?"

"Nap?" Dupree was surprised he nodded out.

Jill giggled. "You have been asleep for almost an hour. We are approaching Salem."

"I was asleep?"

"Unless you snore when you're awake," Michael teased.

"I am so sorry," Dupree offered.

"It must be your nose that made you snore. Can you breathe through your nose?"

"Not much. At least it has stopped throbbing." Dupree reached for an egg roll.

Dupree took a bite of the egg roll and savored the ginger and green onion spiced pork. He chewed slowly and let his taste buds search for more subtle flavors.

Over Michael's shoulder, Dupree spotted the fiery young attorney coming back up the aisle toward him. What does she want? he thought. Maybe she's just changing cars. Don't make eye contact. After his nice chat with the Chens, he was no longer feeling like verbal sparring with her. Dupree looked down and pretended to study the egg roll.

"Excuse me," the familiar voice said.

Dupree grudgingly looked up. He just knew she retreated to regroup and mount a stronger attack.

"Oh, hi." He sat a little straighter.

The Chens looked up at the young woman standing at the end of the table and smiled. She ignored them.

"I just wanted to apologize for our exchange earlier. I had no idea who..."

"So, what a person's Google profile says is more important than just being someone who might be interesting or you could learn from?"

"Well, no. I just didn't..." she stammered.

"Realize that a stranger on a train may have something to offer of value, even if they have two black eyes?"

"That's not what..."

"This is Michael and Jill. They came to the USA thirty-seven years ago. They're on their way to see their new grandson. They've been married forty years. Is that cool or what? Can you imagine?"

"That's nice but..."

"Do you know what they did before they retired?" Dupree pressed on.

"How could I?"

"You see my dear, that is a skill you sorely lack. If you don't cultivate an interest in others, how will you ever be able to read them across the courtroom or conference table? How will you know a person's strengths and weaknesses? The law is a battle of wits, personality, and maneuvering, as much as it is being the best researcher, brief writer, or smartest person in the room. Human nature and the qualities of the good and the bad, the honest and the devious, are always of more value in the heat of a litigation than Who vs Who, 1987. Now, take a look at my friends here. What did they do before they retired?"

"I don't know. I just want to have a chance..."

"You don't care either. Empathy is a very valuable gift. But it is also a tool that can be nurtured and used to great effect in building a strong client-attorney relationship.

"I am giving you a master class in what separates the big fish from the minnows and the pros from the hacks." Dupree pursed his lips and waited. "But you aren't listening; you are just waiting to talk."

"Before, you said you would hire me. Can I arrange to get an interview?"

"What I actually said was, I would have hired you. This was your interview. I have reconsidered my initial impression of you. You need to get knocked around a bit before you are ready for a big firm. If this were an actual interview you would have bombed it, flunked out, blew your chance."

"But why?" The young woman's chin shook and her eyes were filling with tears, either from embarrassment, disappointment, or both. Her confidence and swagger were completely gone. She looked like a high school kid who just lost the mock trial championship on a stupid error.

"I introduced you to my friends, the Chens. I gave you a thumbnail bio, and I asked you what they did before they retired. You not only ignored them and my questions but pushed your own agenda even harder."

"They owned a restaurant." Her voice gave way to panic.

"Oh, no, no, no! Playing into racial stereotypes! That is beyond amateurish, immature, ill-informed, and frankly dangerous. I will not dignify your answer with the correct one.

"Your stop is coming up. When you are waiting for the big important meeting you tried to impress me with, I want you to think about this conversation and see what, if anything, you can recall. What could you put into practice? After all, that is what you hope to do, right, practice law?"

Dupree shook his head and cleared his throat. "I would like to say that it was nice to meet you but you are so self-centered you never bothered to introduce yourself to me, or my friends the Chens, even after I gave you their names. So you see, instead of creating a bond that later could be of benefit when reaching out to me or my firm, you, my dear, are just a nameless stranger on a train that I will soon forget."

The broken girl spun around and ran sobbing up the aisle.

"Oh, Mr. Dupree that was very harsh," Jill said sadly.

"No, my dear Mrs. Chen, that is the world she has chosen. If she can't take my honest counsel and a rather tepid reprimand of her attitude, she will be eaten alive in the real world of lawyers, clerks, and the law. At present she is like a fighter getting in the ring, not realizing someone was about to hit her. This was a great lesson, I hope. Kind of a way of her being brought face to face with what she can expect on a daily basis."

"But you seem to have left that world."

"You can take the lawyer out of the courtroom, but you can't take the courtroom out of the lawyer!" Dupree laughed.

"You certainly seemed to know what to say to that poor young lady."

"If she's smart enough to get it, it's pretty simple stuff, really. Sometimes the simplest things are difficult for brilliant people to understand."

"We all get smart and foolish mixed up at times," Michael said.

"Sometimes I will reread the same passage over and over trying to understand its truth." Jill tapped her Bible with the eraser of her pencil. "The Bible says the Word of God has been made simple to confound the wise."

"Well you're not confounded in your beliefs, and you seem very wise to me," Dupree said gently.

He glanced over at Michael; his face fairly glowed with pride in his bride.

"Oh, you lawyers, always turning people's words around on them. You must have been a very formidable opponent, Mr. Dupree." Michael was nodding with approval.

"I did enjoy the playing of the game."

"I must ask you," Jill looked at Dupree for a long moment before speaking, "Why are you on this train? Why does a man of such obvious professional prowess have two black eyes and a broken nose? I am a good listener if you need a friend."

"Sweetheart, Mr. Dupree must have a lot of friends. I don't think he needs Miss Nosy Rosie prying in his business. Leave the poor man alone."

"Thank you, Michael, but she is a very charming lady, and you are a lucky man. Here is the long and short of it. As you might say in religious terms, I have been born again. I have made a conscious decision to change me, my life, and my environment. I found that my life was in a downward spiral. I had to escape or I would have died. If not by my own hand, a stroke or heart attack would have got me. My head was about to explode. So I walked off. I was hitchhiking, and a guy I got a ride with clobbered me and booted me out of his car. Some wonderful people helped me and insisted I take the train the rest of the way to my destination. So here I am."

"My," said Jill, putting her hand over her mouth. "That was short but very profound. I will be praying for you, Mr. Dupree. I think you have much more to learn. I think God has a plan for you. Be open to it."

"When we stop learning we're dead, right? I am not a believer in much of anything, but if there is a plan I don't know about it, I'd love to take a look." Dupree chuckled. "No offense, I just think I can work things out on my own."

"How's that working for you?" Jill smiled.

"Ouch! Have you ever thought about the Law?"

"Only God's."

"If you want her to stop, just let me know. She is mighty in her faith." Michael nodded and put his arm around his wife. "I don't know what I would have done in my life without her."

"As I said, Michael, you are a lucky man."

"OK, I'll give it a rest. But you can't outrun God. Now eat that last egg roll."

The three friends laughed, but Dupree was more than a little pleased that the conversation would take another path.

"Time for a bathroom break." Dupree stood and stuck the egg roll in his mouth like a cigar. As an afterthought, he turned and picked up his pack.

The restrooms were in the rear of the car near the doors to the exit. When Dupree left the restroom, a flash of green caught his eye through the passageway. He tapped the button to open the door and was hit with a clean blast of fresh air.

The space between cars was open. There were doors about waist high on either side to prevent someone from accidentally falling off the train. Dupree stood to let the cool air wash over him. For a long moment, he stood eyes closed, just taking deep breaths of the rain-washed air.

"Feels good, doesn't it?" a voice asked from behind him.

"It really does. I wish I could put a chair out here," Dupree said brightly but didn't look behind him.

"Mind if I foul the air a bit with a bit of cherry tobacco?"

Dupree turned to face a man of about eighty, holding a straight stem pipe. He wore a grey tweed sport coat and a deep red vest, and atop his head was a matching tweed cap.

"Help yourself," Dupree said, looking into the old man's bright blue eyes.

His eyes nearly gave off sparks. They twinkled with such a mischievous, youthful, possibility.

"Farmer is my name, named such because my father wanted to raise fruit, veg, chickens, and goats. My mother would have none of it! So, I was the constant reminder of what he gave up for her."

"What did he do for a living?"

"His business card read Conrad T. Bennett, Esq. Attorney at Law. The truth of it was, he only had two clients. One, the estate of a filthy rich coal tycoon, who hated his six children and put all his money in a trust, with a pittance of an annual allowance. The other was a woman whose parents were killed in an accident. She was left in a coma for the next thirty years. He saw to it the sanitarium where she was stored got their monthly check."

"Quite a practice." Dupree smiled.

"Every day he would rise at six-thirty, dress, have breakfast, and go to his office at precisely ten minutes to eight. At exactly ten minutes after five each day, he returned home. He did that every day without fail until he shot himself when I was sixteen." The old man stuck the pipe in his mouth and repeatedly tried to light it. After about six attempts he shoved the pipe in his pocket. "I never have got the hang of that damn thing. I can't abide cigarettes though. Would you say I had an oral fixation?"

"Oh, I don't know…" Dupree tried to respond, but Farmer cut him off.

"So as soon as my father was in the ground my mum booked passage for us on a ship to Canada. She was shit for geography, and we landed in Nova Scotia when our destination was the home of her cousin in Victoria, B.C. She died when I was at university so I followed a skirt to Oregon. Her father ran me off, but I settled. Thought I would give law a go. Retired ten years ago, and spend my days riding trains, ferries, and waiting for the grim reaper."

DUPREE'S REBIRTH

Farmer took the pipe out of his pocket and shoved his thumb in the bowl, then turned it upside down and held his lighter under it. He puffed several times and finally, a cloud of bluish-white smoke billowed around his head.

"You look like a man with a story. Let's have it." Farmer crossed his arms and gazed at Dupree.

"I'm off to see the elephant."

"I knew you were a man with a story! Barnum! Ha! Brilliant, go on!"

"I married a woman whose greatest achievement in life was looking good on my arm at dinner parties. We spawned two offspring even more self-absorbed than their protective mother. I considered your father's way out but decided to strike out for the open road. The black eyes are from getting robbed and dumped on the highway in the middle of nowhere. Your story is far more intriguing than mine, but I'm still on the first chapter of the sequel." Dupree grinned at Farmer who was nodding in appreciation of his story.

"Where do you leave this leg of your journey?"

"I heard of a small town in Washington that piqued my interest. I think I'll see what it has to offer. And you?"

"I've decided to ride to the border, then turn around and ride as far south as I can go. Then who knows, maybe I'll head east. My intention is to die on a train."

"You look pretty stout to me," Dupree said.

"To every plan, there is a wrinkle. I may run out of money before I run out of days." Farmer gave an impish grin.

"How old are you, if I might ask?"

"Ninety-three August last. I thought about taking the train east and booking passage on a ship back to Wales. But then I realized there was nothing there that I would know. It was a romantic notion I savored for quite a long while."

"Do you have family in Oregon?"

"No, I've outlived them all. My son died at sixty-eight last year. He had one son who died in Iraq. Damn stupid war that. My wife has been gone for forty years, nearly twice as long as we were married. You know, if you live long enough numbers get to be quite fascinating."

"It seems you have lived an incredible life. Have you ever thought of writing a memoir?"

"Too much work. Besides, it would end up lies, exaggerations, and scandalous truths."

"Besides your charming family, what has your life been about?"

"I, too, was an attorney. I loved the game, you know, besting my opponent, but I began to wonder what it profited anyone other than clients who already had cheated, stolen, and manipulated more than their fair share already. I began to feel for the losers. It began to really weigh heavily on my mind."

"Oh dear, you were growing a conscience. If you are to be your kind of lawyer you can't have one of those if you are going to continue. I always fought for the little guy. David versus Goliath, Mary Pickerin' against the Great Pacific Lumber Company. I got her three million. Her husband fell into a plywood pulp machine. The foreman removed the safety rail, under orders from the mill manager. I grabbed them by the balls and never let go until they screamed uncle! God, I miss it."

Dupree nodded in agreement. "The fight is what I'll miss. I just seemed, in the end, to always be on the wrong side. Tell me something, Farmer. In all your years, what is the one thing you can tell me to get me through?"

The old man didn't hesitate a second. "Always kick 'em when they're down because if you don't, they might get up and kill you." The old man winked at Dupree, banged his pipe against the outside wall of the door, and went back into the train.

Dupree looked down at a mangy, black German Shepherd barking for all it's worth at the passing train. He thought of Don Quixote and yelled: "Give it up!"

Chapter 9

It seemed an eternity since Dupree boarded the train. He felt the need to stretch his legs, more than the occasional trip to the restroom. After about ten minutes he followed Farmer's lead and entered the adjourning car, his goal being to walk the full length of the train in both directions.

It felt good to walk more than a few feet. Dupree tried to estimate the length of the cars as he approached the end of the first complete car he passed through. His math was derailed when a massive woman in yoga pants was overtaken by the shopping bag she was trying to remove from the overhead storage.

The bag full of chips, several open bags of candy, a half-full liter bottle of Pepsi, three empty Gatorade bottles, and a hand full of candy bars fell, emptying its contents on the heads of a pair of sleeping, dread-locked travelers.

The pair leaped to their feet yelling like the sky was falling.

Yoga pants returned their shouts with strong admonishments to not wake her baby.

"You woke my baby!" the blond, bearded hippie yelled back at her. "You okay, babe?" he asked his companion.

She nodded with a spacey stare, and settled back under her poncho and closed her eyes.

"I need my stuff," Yoga yelled.

"Dude, you've got way more processed poison than three people would need in a lifetime. Let it go. Get some fruit, vegetables, organic if possible, and begin to cleanse your body and spirit of the poisons you have been abusing it with. A bowl of ganja would certainly help with your anger issues. You are a walking time bomb just waiting for a heart attack or stroke. Let it go, learn to chill. Sorry I shattered the environment with noise, but your monsoon of artificial flavor, colors and processed sugar totally shattered my REM sleep." He swept the various foodstuffs from his seat, sat down and pulled part of the poncho over his shoulders.

The woman threw herself to the floor and began frantically scooping up the candy. Like a scene from a Dickens orphanage, she snatched and grabbed like the bits of butterscotch and multicolored Jolly Ranchers were the only thing between her and starvation.

Dupree was given no choice but to wait until the woman was satisfied she retrieved the last peanut M&M and Skittle from the floor. As he stood patiently waiting, he watched the people observing the scene pointing and giggling as her top rode up, exposing her soft, white, stretch-marked belly wobbling from side to side as she worked feverishly.

When she finally was able to pull herself up from her knees and to a standing position, she scowled and looked from one grinning passenger to the next. "I hope you're amused! This is my lunch."

No one spoke. Her glare eventually landed on Dupree. He just shrugged and moved to get by her.

"Thanks for the help," the woman growled as he tried to squeeze past.

"Excuse me," Dupree said, softly pulling himself forward with the back of a seat.

She made no effort to move.

The next three cars were free of incident and Dupree walked along smiling and nodding at the mostly friendly passengers. A conductor stood a few feet from the end of the third car and glared at Dupree as he approached.

"End of the line." The conductor's tone said, "Turn around."

"What's up there?"

"Baggage and the engine."

"Oh, right. Is it possible to see the engine?" Dupree asked.

"No."

"Alright. How many cars are on this train?"

"Six passenger, three freight."

It was apparent to Dupree the conductor was not interested in him or his questions. "Thank you."

"Uh-huh."

With reversed direction and renewed dedication, Dupree headed back to find car number six. As he walked from car to car, it was like being on a different train. A new set of faces greeted him even as he went through the cars he already visited. Upon entering the fifth car, he spotted a staircase. There was no posting of any kind so he went up the stairs to find a nearly empty observation car. The view was far nicer than the seats he previously occupied. He decided to stay.

The People magazine Dupree read was left on the seat by a previous passenger. As he caught up on a world he was pretty much oblivious to, the train jerked hard and someone slammed against Dupree in an attempt to keep their balance.

"Whoa! You alright?" Dupree said, trying to right a woman in a tight headscarf.

She slid into the seat across the table as the train rocked from side to side.

"Where are you going?" Dupree thought he might need to help her get back to her seat.

"I'm running away from home." A whimsical smile gently touched her lips.

The truth of her statement made it clear; it wasn't an attempt at humor. There was an undercurrent to the frail woman's first words to Dupree.

"Me too," he replied.

"Did you pack a lunch? Most runaways forget to bring something along for later. When I was a little girl I ran away from home in the third grade. Instead of going to school, I went to the park. I played on the swings, climbed all over the Jungle Gym, can we still say that?"

"Do you really care?" Dupree reflected back.

"Not really."

"Me either."

"I had such a wonderful time," she continued. "I made sandcastles. I even tried to play on the teeter-totter, but that was futile." She chuckled softly. "I played until I grew very hungry. I figured that it must be time for school to be out, so I started back home. When I went through the back door into the kitchen my mother was standing at the sink.

"She gave me a perplexed look. 'What are you doing here?' she asked.

"Am I late?"

"No, three hours early!"

"Did you learn a lesson?" Dupree questioned.

"I did. I remembered it until I was eighteen and ran off with a boy who played guitar and wrote songs with deep, philosophical lyrics. They actually were pure piffle, but it was all rainbows, daisies, and Volkswagen buses in search of peace, love, and harmony in those days.

"It lasted all the way to Santa Cruz. On the first night, we made love on the beach in the shelter of the dunes. When I awoke on the bus, my clothes, the guitar player, and the money stashed in my Kotex box were gone."

"So this is your third attempt at running away," Dupree said, hoping she would continue.

"No, there was my first husband, Ruben. We met in a Psych class. He was so brilliant. After being married to him for six months, I understood why he knew so much about psychology. He was psychotic!" She moved her scarf back just above her temple to expose an indentation the size of a quarter and about as deep. "Ball peen hammer. That was runaway number three. I went all the way to Vermont to make sure he didn't find me. I turned twenty-one working on a maple syrup commune, pregnant with Ruben's baby. It was born with too many birth defects to survive. They wouldn't even let me see it. So I don't even know if it was a boy or girl. Just as well. I needed to grow up."

Dupree smiled but didn't speak. He had no words.

"I'm Mary Ann."

"Dupree."

"I didn't mean to blather on, but when your clock is winding down it seems you have more to say than you have time or people for. Where are you headed?"

"White Owl, Washington."

"Oh, I went to the Summer Solstice Festival there. It is a mystical village as I recall. Lots of positive energy, as we used to say."

"What do you say now?"

"I'm dying."

"How long?" Dupree felt a real connection with this frail woman.

"A month tops."

"So where are you going?"

"Lake Louise. It is the most beautiful place I ever saw. I used to tell people it had water to die for. I want to see if I was right." Mary Ann laughed until she coughed violently.

"Can I get you anything?" Dupree asked as the cough subsided.

"A full-body transplant? Relax, this will pass." She paused a three count then said, "and so will I."

The black humor seemed as natural to her as breathing.

"So who did you run away from?" Dupree asked.

"You first."

"What do you mean?"

"Haven't you heard? Dying people have a special gift. It's in your eyes, Dupree. We are fellow travelers, except you're healthy. Emotionally I have a feeling you might be a cracked vessel."

"Actually I am cracked, but it's letting the poison out. I am more alive and happier than I can ever remember being, except maybe when I was a kid."

"What's your secret?" Mary Ann asked.

"Maybe it's just knowing when enough is enough. Like you and Ruben. There comes a time when your self-preservation is more important than anything else. I reached that point and just took off. I didn't plan it, I didn't prepare, just turned left when I was supposed to, expected to, ought to, have turned right. This train is full of run-tos and run-aways.

"I met a kid of twenty-three and an old guy of ninety-three, and both of them are on a journey. They knew exactly where they were bound and I don't mean a town. I mean, where they wanted, needed, to be. You're on the same kind of journey. That lake is the race's end. The old man wants to die on a train. The kid wants to sing his own songs, and this train is the conduit we are all passing through.

"The difference is I am just starting my journey, feeling my way, finding where I belong and just enjoying the ride. The question is, are the three of you road signs along my way? Who was it that said when you don't know where you're going, any road will take you there?"

"I bet you were a trip in the sixties."

"I wasn't born yet," Dupree teased.

"Well, you would have been."

"So who did you run away from this time?"

"This time is different," Mary Ann began. "This time I am running to not hurt others."

"How so?"

"I don't want my wonderful husband and three kids to see me wither, all doped out on morphine, and die an ashen gray skeleton. When I left a month ago, except for the Chemo Scarf Chic," she struck a pose, palms out behind her head, "I looked and acted normal."

"Where's home?"

"North Carolina. You?"

"L.A."

"Same question. Who'd you run away from?"

"Why am I telling you all this stuff?" Dupree stopped dead.

"Because I don't matter, I'm dying, you'll never see me again. You need to. You know, there is great freedom in the intimacy of strangers. I've had this conversation, or one like it, a hundred times in the last month. They were people who have jobs, families, dreams, and secrets that no one knows about. Along comes a dying woman and they spill their innermost secrets and don't look back.

"Look how deep we've gotten in less than five minutes. You already know me better than my next-door neighbor, and the folks who come for barbecue back home.

"You know what I wish? I wish I could see the healing after I leave. I'm like an all at once shrink, priest, and best friend they never had."

"I left a wife and two kids," Dupree said flatly.

"They love you?"

"No."

"Wow. You didn't even have to think."

"Didn't need to."

"Why are you so sure?"

"Because I don't love them. It is a horrible thing to admit, I know. But, I've had a thousand miles on and off to think it through. I should have taken the higher road years ago. Probably in the first couple of years I was married, before kids."

"You think they are looking for you?" Dupree asked.

"Don't care. This is about me."

"That's kind of selfish, isn't it?"

"Look who's talking! You rich?"

"I'm wealthy by most standards, I guess."

"And you just walked off."

"That's right."

"Lord, you are a miracle!"

Dupree laughed heartily. "How do you figure?"

"Because no one gives up money unless they are a true believer."

"I don't believe in anything," Dupree replied.

"I don't mean in a spiritual sense. I mean you are beyond committed. Kind of like the story of the chicken and the hog who questioned who loved the farmer more. It was the hog, and you're the hog."

"I don't get it."

"The chicken was dedicated to the farmer because it lays an egg every day. But the hog is fully committed because he provides the bacon."

"So what you're saying is, 'I have gone whole hog?'" Dupree grinned.

"Very good!" Mary Ann clapped her hands.

"We will be arriving in Portland Station in five minutes. Passengers continuing on will have a forty-five-minute layover. Those of you leaving us, be sure and collect all your belongings before exiting the train, and thank you for traveling Amtrak!"

"That'll be me!" Mary Ann said, "I'm collecting some meds and hunkering down until the nausea passes. Nice to meet you. I hope you find what you're looking for."

"I wish you peace," Dupree said softly.

"Don't get all mushy with me. I chose this trip. I am going out on my terms."

Neither spoke until the train came to a stop.

"See ya around, Dupree." Mary Ann picked up her small satchel and walked away.

Portland was enormous compared to the small town stops the train made since Dupree came aboard. With the exception of Salem, this was the only station that seemed to have history. Dupree stood and changed to the opposite side of the table when Mary Ann left.

He looked out the window in time to see her turn, find him and wave. He returned her good-bye and smiled. A few moments later he saw Foster James.

He stood guitar case in one hand and a backpack in the other. Clinging to his arm was a girl. She too held a backpack. She was dressed in black tights, a short skirt, a long gray sweater, and on her head, she wore a black beret. Her long blond hair nearly reached her waist. She turned slightly and Dupree could see a very plain, very pale face, partially hidden by large, round, black-rimmed glasses. If the kid from Merced wanted the archetypical, artsy-fartsy, bohemian girlfriend, looks-wise anyway, he hit a home run.

It didn't take hearing words for Dupree to tell that they were planning a life of music, art, and hipness, all on the platform of the Portland, Oregon train station. The only question was if he was going home with her to meet her parents. Good for them, he thought, as they walked away arm in arm.

Hundreds of people filled the station. In the distance, Dupree could see shops, restaurants, and an information booth. He decided he would go for a walk since the announcement said they would have forty-five minutes in the station. That would be plenty of time, he thought, to get a fresh, real cup of coffee, and perhaps a magazine or sandwich.

"Would you mind saving this seat for me?" Dupree asked the man across the aisle.

"I'll see what I can do. No promises. Here." The man tossed Dupree his coat and umbrella. "That should do the trick."

"Thanks."

"Yep." The man went back to his tattered paperback.

The platform smelled of diesel and humanity. Everywhere people swirled, dodged, and bumped into each other. Uncooperative, wobbly-wheeled suitcases brought forward progress to a halt as hurried passengers cursed and fought them. Camouflage uniformed military personnel, toting huge duffel bags, moved straight ahead with determined movement through the crowd.

Dupree adjusted his pack to ride comfortably across his midsection and rested his arm across the top. He pressed through the crowd like a battered salmon swimming upstream. Once free of the congestion, it could have been in any mall in America. The need to shop in transportation centers always baffled Dupree.

Was the impulsive urge to buy so strong that humanity could be tempted with all manner seemingly irresistible products, even as they rushed to catch a plane or train? The marketing guru's plans seemed to be working.

As Dupree stopped to get his bearing and determined which way to go, he could see from where he stood the choices of Dutch Brothers, Peet's, and the ever-present Starbucks. Do people really need three kinds of coffee at a train station? Whatever happened to diners with waiters in paper caps and white aprons pouring strong coffee into heavy white mugs? The image from an old black and white movie came rushing back to Dupree.

The windmill logo won out and Dupree bought coffee from Dutch Bothers. The choices for a sandwich were narrower, but the proximity of Togo's made it the easy choice. Dupree found he enjoyed being an average consumer. Now, for a newspaper, or a copy of The New Yorker.

To find a newsstand Dupree was forced to walk considerably farther than for food. The tiny kiosk of magazines, gum, and papers was almost missed. Dupree approached with the anticipation of getting some substantial reading material instead of the mindless dreck he tried to wade through earlier.

His breath seemed to explode silently inward as Dupree read the headline: Nationwide Manhunt Continues for Prominent L.A. Attorney. He stood motionless. His escape was so personal, the load lifted so completely, he hadn't considered the ramifications.

Of course they would search for him, of course the news would cover it, of course appeals would be made for his return. As he paid for the paper, he caught a glimpse of himself in the mirror behind the counter in the little shop. He looked down at the stock portrait of himself below the headline in the paper. Four days' growth of beard, two black eyes, and not a drop of expensive barber salon product in his hair, it would take more than a casual glance to make a connection. All the same, he thought, something must be done.

Only in an old train station can you still find a telephone booth. This remnant of pre-cellular communications was like a beacon of hope to Dupree. He put his sandwich and coffee on the tiny metal shelf, and the newspaper under his arm.

He took the handful of change from his pocket and deposited the required amount into the slot. The eleven numbers buttons were pushed in rapid succession.

Three rings and the call was answered.

"Give me Ingrid," Dupree demanded.

"Mister…"

"Do it!" Dupree cut in.

"Yes sir, please hold on."

"This is Ingrid." The strong in-charge voice of Dupree's secretary came on the line. She was a granite pyre in his life. She was never sick; she never took time off. Dupree, the firm, and her job were all that mattered in her world. If she was married, had children, a house, apartment, pets, or a dying mother, Dupree never knew, or cared.

She got a thousand-dollar bonus on her birthday and Christmas. She bought him lunch, made coffee, took dictation, assigned research to the clerks, and bought his wife and children Christmas, birthday, graduation, and anniversary gifts.

"Dupree."

"Oh my God, where are you?" She shattered the veil of formality. "I, I mean, we have been worried sick!"

"Take a message, would you?"

"Of course, yes sir. Ready. What is it?"

"Tell Mr. Hutchinson to see the dogs are called off." Dupree slammed the receiver down in its cradle.

Martin Hutchinson, senior partner and grandson of the firm's founder, was as close to a friend as Dupree had. They were not laugh and joke, play golf, or go to a ballgame friends, they were friendly trusted coworkers. If Dupree ever needed to confide in someone, it would be Hutchinson. In twenty years, it only happened once. Then it turned out to be unnecessary. They shared a stiff drink when Martin Hutchinson's father, Vernon, died, but no tears were shed.

He would know what Dupree wanted. He would personally make the call to the Chief of Police. The calls to the influential media connections the firm kept on a comfortable retainer would be assigned to one of the other partners under a need to know, and in this case, nothing, basis.

With any luck, the story would be dead by the next twenty-four-hour news cycle. A statement so obtuse, you would not be able to find meaning with a microscope, will be released by the news outlets that will put their subsidiaries completely off the story. The police will shift their focus to a more sensational case and Dupree's disappearance will just fall off the radar, with any luck.

Dupree quickly returned to his seat in the observation car. It was no longer empty so he moved several rows forward. He preferred the anonymity of the back-right corner seat. It was not to be.

Within a few minutes of their departure, an announcement was made that the train entered the State of Washington. Dupree took his ticket from his pocket and reviewed his itinerary. In Tacoma, he would leave the train and catch a bus to the Okanogan

Highlands in the northeast corner of the state, and his destination, White Owl.

"Ticket please." The conductor began repeating as he entered the car.

"How long to Tacoma?" Dupree asked as his ticket was punched.

The conductor looked at his watch "Three hours, thirty-eight minutes."

"Wow." Dupree expressed how impressed he was.

"Give or take thirty or forty minutes." The conductor grinned and moved on.

The newspaper article was vague about the details of Dupree's disappearance. As to plan, the focus of the search for the first two days was south of Los Angeles. It told of his car being found at the rest stop. A plea was made for anyone stopping on the day of his disappearance to report any sighting of Dupree. A woman reported she saw him walking his dog. A trucker said he saw him talking to a woman in a pickup truck about three in the afternoon. The third, and to Dupree the funniest report, was that he was in an altercation with a group of bikers. The cause was not known, but there was a lot of yelling and screaming shortly before he was rescued by a man in a Ford Bronco.

None were credible witnesses. If Dupree read the article first, he probably would never have made the call to his office.

His wife Diane, in typical overdramatic fashion, spoke of her love for her husband, the brilliant lawyer, philanthropist, and past president of Hill Glen Golf and Country Club. She asked that anyone with any information please come forward so that her college sweetheart, husband, and loving, inspirational father to her exceptional children, could come home to them. If the worst should have happened, she knew he would be in a better place. Then according to the reporter, she collapsed into the arms of her grieving son, Eric.

"Oh, brother," Dupree said aloud.

The article went on to give quotes from Martin Hutchinson and two of the younger partners at the firm. They spoke, from statements obviously prepared by the PR department, about "the dedication Dupree showed to the law and his unflinching determination to get to the truth, in every case, no matter how small, or seemingly trivial they may seem to the rest of the world. He fought for them as if they were the biggest corporate case their firm took on."

"My God, I wish I could fire whoever wrote that crap," Dupree muttered.

For the next hour, Dupree read the rest of the paper cover to cover. It wasn't that he was particularly interested in the twelve obituaries or the premiere of this year's Ladies Garden Society Grand Tour. He wanted something to get his mind off the fact that his great escape could be scuttled by his own recklessness.

How many people did he tell that he was a lawyer from L.A? How many people did he tell he was an attorney? Weavers would never give him away; neither would Mary Ann, but the fame-hungry Foster James may report seeing him as a way to get his name, songs, and new band in the news. The old lawyer could hardly remember his own name, so by the time he found someone to tell, if indeed he bothered, he would never remember the details.

Dupree took a deep breath and sighed. What am I worried about, he thought. He didn't use any credit cards, or stay anywhere they required ID. He got off the train twice. He was wearing clothes that didn't belong to him a week ago. No suit, no tie, and no expensive Italian shoes. His hair was no longer plastered down with gel, not shaving produced a fairly-thick salt and pepper covering, and then there were the black eyes. Dupree grinned; the way he looked he would get kicked out of the lobby of his own building. He told himself to relax, enjoy the ride, and let the chips fall where they may.

As a young lawyer, he dealt with the estate of a man who disappeared from his greedy heirs. Leland Johan Nilsson had only been missing five days when his daughter, her dim wit jock brother, and their overbearing, spendaholic mother sat in his small office and demanded access to Nilsson's bank accounts, stock portfolio, and business assets.

The problem was none of their names appeared on any documents pertaining to the missing man's money.

"But I'm his wife!" Dupree remembered the fiery redhead screaming across his paper and folder laden desk.

"I know daddy wouldn't want me to do without." The daughter laid on the deep cleavage, false eyelash batting, sex for favors hard-sell on the young Dupree.

"What about our Lakers tickets? The deposit is due next week!" Who cares about dad when there is basketball at stake? The son was not a bit subtle in his concerns.

To Dupree's delight, nothing could be done for them. Without the knowledge of his distraught family members, Leland Nilsson prepared files, kept in the office, with the strict instruction that in case of his mysterious disappearance or sudden death, his wife and children were to receive absolutely nothing.

The State of California requires a person who simply disappears must remain so for a period of seven years before they can be legally declared dead. There was no indication of abduction, no ransom note, there was no evidence of foul play in either his office or home. He attended a party with his wife the night before his disappearance, and according to friends and associates, was in rare form, cracking jokes, telling stories and being in better spirits than they had seen him in months. He even danced with his wife! So, suicide was ruled out by one and all.

The case sludged on for six years. Through the marriage and divorce of his daughter twice, four DUI arrests of the angry, sports betting, loser son, and the sordid affairs of his wife and the subsequent repossession of the family home because, oddly enough, it was solely in her name.

On the anniversary of his disappearance, a registered letter arrived requiring the signature of his new partner Dupree. In the letter was a photo of Mr. Nilsson in a pair of khaki shorts and a Hawaiian shirt. His arm was around a beautiful, considerably younger, large breasted, dark-skinned Polynesian woman. The letter stated that he would like all his assets, whatever they may be, transferred to the account number attached in Bora Bora, and a request that the process be started for the divorce from his unfaithful wife, and complete power of attorney for Dupree, duly processed and notarized by the U.S. Deputy Consulate of Tahiti, James, E. Kincaid.

Everything was legal, above board and, after a phone call and follow up letter to Mr. Kincaid, was duly processed, served, and finalized under California law.

The case was a great source of pride and amusement over the years. When Dupree had a drink too many and someone complained about a spouse, kids or business partner, he was convinced it was the ultimate template for executing a perfect separation of assets and relationships.

All these years later Dupree was riding on a train, the perpetrator of a disappearance, and left with everything he owned in both his and his wife's name. For Dupree, it didn't matter. When the time comes, he thought, things will sort themselves out.

The connection to the eastbound bus was a little bit more complicated than the Weavers explained, but after two hours waiting in a drafty bus station, his bus was called.

The bus was almost completely filled when Dupree climbed up the three worn steps. He found a seat next to a woman who stunk of tobacco and sour whiskey. She was sound asleep or passed out. As the bus pulled into the dark Washington night, the woman rolled slightly in the seat and put her head on Dupree's shoulder. He rotated in his seat, trying to rouse her enough to get her back on her side of the armrest, but instead, she fell face-first into his lap.

Across the narrow aisle, two Hispanic men laughed loudly, drawing the attention of two women in front of them.

"Get a room would ya!" one woman called out at Dupree.

The two men laughed even louder. Dupree grabbed the woman by the shoulders and roughly shoved her against the window. She snorted, slumped down in the seat, and began to snore.

Dupree turned back toward the two men, each of which was waiting with a high five. Dupree slapped their palms and laughed.

"It's going to be a long ride!"

"No habla Ingles." The men returned with big smiles.

Dupree could tell they were lying, but just shook his head and smiled.

Mile after mile rolled by and Dupree drifted off to sleep. The bus stopped frequently to pick up and let off passengers. He would open one eye look out the window and try to read the name of the depot. Most of the time the stop was at a crossroads gas station or small town Post office.

"White Owl. Next stop White Owl. We won't be here long enough for a rest stop but there will be a chance for coffee and bathrooms in about another thirty minutes. In an emergency, you can use the toilet on the bus. I repeat, *in an emergency*." The driver paused as a woman near the back shouted something. He didn't hear, didn't understand, or care, and continued. "Is there anyone getting off in White Owl?"

Dupree raised his hand.

"OK, then we'll stop."

The bus pulled up in front of the White Owl Post Office. "All off for White Owl."

Dupree stood and climb out into the aisle. The drunk woman took the opportunity to slump over onto his empty seat. Dupree made his way to the front of the bus.

"Any luggage?"

"Just this."

"Thanks for traveling with us today." The driver's words couldn't have been any more lifeless if he was sedated.

Dupree didn't respond. He took the three steps off the bus and in one giant step entered a whole new life.

A giant belch of exhausted signaled the bus's departure. As the bus rolled down the street, Dupree crossed the street to escape the cloud of exhaust. There were very few cars on the street. He looked up and down the block and admired the old buildings and their early twentieth-century filigree.

His journey was over. For good or bad, this is the end of the line. Dupree took a long deep breath of the crisp clean air.

"Looks like a nice little town. A fresh start, a new beginning." Dupree smiled. "You sound like the narrator of an old black and white movie." Dupree chuckled.

With a big smile and a heart full of promise, Dupree walked toward the nearest corner. At the corner, he looked up at the street sign. He was standing at the intersection of Fulfillment Street and Opportunity Avenue. Dupree shook his head. "If that's not some kind of a sign…"

To his left on the next block was a coffee shop. Quarter Moon Café the sign read. "This calls for a big piece of pie and a cup of coffee. Good place to start mixing with the natives and find a place to stay." Dupree started for the café.

Life is a funny journey at times. Fate shoves us this way and that, without explanation or warning. A journey that began with the choice between a right or left turn forever changed Dupree's life. Once again, the choice to turn left on Opportunity would be just that. There was no way he could know that in another block he would find Contentment.

THE END

DUPREE'S REWARD

Exclusive sample from Book 2

Chapter One

The Quarter Moon Café was at the intersection of Opportunity and Inspiration. It was a kind of White Owl's *un*official city hall. The mayor and council members would argue, plead, and compromise on the issues affecting White Owl. In election years, a thick black strip of duct tape divided the café in half, Dems on one side, Republicans on the other. The owner forbad, under threat of expulsion until after November tenth, anyone heard arguing partisan politics. The rest of the time it was a happy gathering of locals and the occasional visitor. Good-humored teasing and strong hot coffee were served up with the best-baked goods in the county. The Quarter Moon boasted a long, proud history in White Owl.

In 1927, the Mayflower Bakery opened for the benefit of the Cornish lumbermen who migrated south from British Columbia in hopes of settling on a land offering that failed at the end of World War I. The idea being, the returning Doughboys would jump at the chance of owning a piece of the beautiful highlands country. Few came and fewer stayed. The winters were fierce, the rain was frequent, and the roads in and out were nearly impassable half the year.

The Mayflower's claim to fame was the meaty, flaky crusted pastries that Mrs. Bridgette Thompson made up each morning. The lumbermen, sheepmen, and locals would line up and hand over a dime or two and walk away with their lunch or a tasty breakfast. When the morning offerings ran out the bakery produced pies, cakes, and loaves of hearty, brown bread.

The Mayflower was a thriving concern until one morning in May 1933, when Mrs. Thompson was found on the floor of the kitchen, a burning tray of her beloved Lady Finger cookies in the oven, another scattered all around her. The doctor said that her heart simply exploded.

The building sat empty for a year or two until the wife of a local land agent thought she would give the bakery business a go. After all, her children loved her cookies, and friends often comment that they "never had anything like her scones." The truth be told, the children would have been just as happy to have eaten the sugary dough from the bowl, just as much as the over-baked version served up by their mother on Saturday afternoons. The friends, who said they never tasted anything like her scones, didn't mean it in a good way. They often asked if they could take theirs home for later. They were always given another as well. Both only made it as far as the nearest rubbish bin.

Betty's Bunnery, as she named it, only lasted six months. At that time there were only two repeat customers. Betty's husband came once a day to check on her and get a cup of coffee, but his visit often ended in loud tear-filled arguments over why he never asked for any of her baked offerings.

The second was a woman new to White Owl who came for a dozen buns. Betty said she didn't have any at the moment. The woman left bemused but said she would return, and she did a week later. When she requested another dozen buns Betty was forced to admit she didn't know how to make buns.

"Why is it called a 'Bunnery' then?" the woman asked, dumbfounded.

"Bunnery seemed to go well with Betty."

"What about bakery? Since you do have baked goods," the woman suggested.

A flustered Betty admitted that she never thought of that.

That Bunnery closed a week later.

The little building was again abandoned. Over time the windows were knocked out by local hooligans and angry drunks who took their rage out on the poor little bakery with empty ale bottles. A few years later the land agent died and Betty followed her children to Ohio.

In the summer of 1940, Mr. Oswald Ming and his wife May came to White Owl. The clever Mr. Ming went to the county seat and obtained the property, building and all, for the ten years of back taxes owed, two hundred and ten dollars. All summer long the Ming's did repairs and painted. The tables and chairs were replaced with booths. The display cases were replaced by stools and a counter for quick lunch patrons. In the fall the newly converted building opened as a sparkling new, red and gold Chinese restaurant, The New Moon Café.

For twenty years the Mings served up chop suey, egg drop soup, and chicken chow mein to the grateful residents of White Owl who tired of the heavy meat and potato fare that graced their tables at home. On the twentieth anniversary of the opening of The New Moon, Oswald and May announced they would retire. The next day they packed their car and headed for San Francisco. They sold the property for twelve thousand dollars to Peter Twillham, an investor with great hopes for the little town.

The sixties were a time of change for White Owl. The new highway brought curious vacationers in their station wagons and camp trailers. Davis's Grocery became Big D Supermarket. The gas station's two pumps were replaced by a shiny new six pump Flying A franchise. The New Moon was replaced by a succession of hamburger joints, diners, and The Chicken Coop, which served omelets in the morning and fried chicken for lunch and dinner.

State snowplows cleared the highway, and the county bought White Owl snow removal equipment, making the little community accessible year-round. A wealthy member of a positive thinking cult, called Thinking is Creating, built a large meeting hall, and a complex of small cabins for reflection and meditation. The cult held quarterly retreats in White Owl for years, until the leader ran off with the wife of one of the cult's biggest contributors. The faithful tried to press on, but without the charismatic founder, there wasn't enough positive thinking to keep the creativity going. The hall and complex were sold to a big church in Walla Walla and continues to this day as a summer camp and conference center, adding to the local economy several times a year.

The Chicken Coop closed in 1969. The Seattle holding company that owned the property saw it as just another investment, tax-write off property. The building was leased to a woman who ran a consignment and thrift shop through the seventies and into the eighties. As styles came and went, and the town grew around her, Colleene kept The Clothes Closet going. A department store opened in 1982 and for a time the townspeople thought the second-hand clothes were below their dignity, until the recession in the mid-eighties. The department store closed up. They donated everything left after the big closing sale to The Clothes Closet. Once again, the town folks found recycled clothes fit just fine. The Clothes Closet finally closed in 1988, when Colleene retired.

There was talk of tearing the building down. The value of the corner lot increased considerably over the years. What was once part of the muddy road in front of The Mayflower Bakery was now a row of paved parking spaces, enlarging the lot.

Several offers were made. The land, it seemed, was worth far more than the building. One of the serious bids came from ARCO. They intended to tear down the building and build an AM/PM twenty-four-hour gas and convenience store. Unfortunately for them, Gerard Nickerson sat on the city council. His sister and her husband owned the old Flying A gas station, where they ran a small store with gas pumps. The city council refused the permit and the ARCO project was scuttled.

The Seattle holding company was scooped up by investment bankers who invested heavily in ENRON. They filed bankruptcy when their overextended empire folded with ENRON. The Clothes Closet building was taken over by the town for taxes and though it was listed at a fair price, it sat empty for years, a white and powder blue eyesore.

In the late spring of 1999, Mike Kelly and his best friend, Teddy Auckland, petitioned the city council to hold an outdoor music festival in the meadow north of town. Named on the permit application as the White Owl Summer Solstice Music and Art Festival, no one could have imagined what those seven words would mean to the town and its inhabitants.

Mike and Teddy proved to be a pair of charmingly humble entrepreneurs. The first year, there were around two thousand attendees, twenty-five vendors, and six musical acts that ranged from an acoustic Celtic group, a bluegrass band, Native American dancers, a gospel quartet from Alabama called the Sonshine Boys and a couple of a little past their prime rock and roll bands.

The audience ranged from old retired couples in motor homes to long-haired vagabonds in beat-up old Volvos. The festival was a great success. The whole mood of the town seemed to lift with the influx of new blood, and all the businesses in town saw a mid-summer spike in revenues.

In front of The Clothes Closet, a middle-aged hippie sold large colorful tapestries, Seattle Seahawks blankets, and probably a lot of marijuana. The Sheriff's Department turned a blind eye, not wanting to seem reactionary or unfriendly to all the money coming into town. Apart from a couple of local kids that the giant party proved to just be too much for, resulting in their arrest for a drunken ride through town in the back of a pickup, the weekend proved to be a huge success without incident.

The next year, Mike and Teddy were welcomed back with open arms. With a larger budget and the rave reviews by vendors and festival-goers alike, the festival grew to a two-day affair. The bill included fifteen acts, most of which were well known in the Americana and Jam Band world.

The Festival ticket sales topped ten thousand. The venue extended into the side of the Hamilton Mountain basin, which proved to be an amazing natural amphitheater. There were so many vendors that applied the city offered to close down Main Street and have an open-air market. The promoters were delighted and willingly shared the revenues from the booths fifty/fifty with the city, a move that guaranteed Mayor Chatom's reelection that November.

That year, four college girls from Portland loaded up a yellow Pinto station wagon with sleeping bags, an army surplus tent, provisions for the weekend adventure, and set out for White Owl. Nancy owned the car and was the mother hen of the group. Halley rode shotgun and played navigator. Misha sat in the back seat and complained. Later, the other three girls would argue over who invited her. Then there was Dara. She was the sparkler on the cake. Just like her name's pronounced, Dare-uh was the first to take a dare, the first one in the pool, talk to a stranger, or approach a handsome young man across the room. She would sing, tell stories, and roll down the window and stick her head out, just to feel the wind in her hair. She drove Misha crazy, but Dara Landry was the glue that held the group together.

The girls seemed to be the essence of the festival, young, outgoing, and very pretty. When the heat of the day got to be too much, they shed their blouses or t-shirts and wore only their bikini tops and shorts. Dara seemed to float through the crowd in her pale-yellow bikini top and flowing, cotton, gypsy skirt. Her long, curly, raven hair bounced behind her and caught the eye of all the young men and some of the older ones. Unaffected, and unaware of her natural beauty, her lovely smile greeted anyone she made eye contact with. A few times she was approached by young men full of themselves and on the prowl for female conquests.

Her friendly but confident whoa, big boy, cool your jets! was never condescending, and left their fragile male egos intact.

When offered drugs or alcohol from a well-meaning partier, her charming 'I'm good' conveyed a happiness in her sobriety that was both non-judgmental and understood.

In the evening, after the last act of the day left the stage, the girls wandered from campfire to campfire enjoying the impromptu jam sessions and sing-alongs. Once or twice Dara's strong, crystal clear, vocal rose above the crowd and they faded away, letting her sing a verse, chorus, or both. She would smile, stand, and curtsy to the applause of the group circled around the fire.

The second day of the festival, Halley and Dara strolled the outdoor market on Main Street. The crafts, antiques, and variety of food items fascinated Dara, not the items, or offerings themselves, but the way the vendors displayed their wares. The food items were of particular interest to her and she took every opportunity to taste the samples and examine the packaging. The manner in which the cookies, brownies, hummus, and loaves of artisan bread were transferred from vendor to buyer fascinated her.

Long after Halley tired of the booths and returned to the music meadow, Dara chatted and questioned the food vendors about where they were from, how they transported their goods, and what, if any, health and safety regulations they were subject to. Even the most secretive vendor would finally be worn down by the pretty girl with the dazzling smile into giving up the names of their suppliers of bags and banners, and one organic jam alchemist even gave up his secret recipe.

Instead of returning to her friends and the music, Dara walked around town deep in thought. She was so intrigued by the street market she was convinced it was just the kind of life she would love to live. That night, snuggled down in her sleeping bag, she found it hard to sleep. Her mind raced with the images and words of the afternoon's vendors.

On the way home the next day, Dara announced that next year she would have a booth in the street fair.

"What, selling your million and one hair clips?" Misha groaned.

"No, I will bring banana nut bread and chocolate zucchini bread. There was nothing like my zucchini bread, and my banana nut bread is way better than anything anybody had!"

"You don't know anything about selling stuff at a street market. I bet there's a lot to it," Nancy chimed in.

"She can do it!" Halley said, cutting off the objections of her friends. "You should have seen her. She was in her own world. You could almost hear the wheels turning in her head. Those poor people won't know what hit them. I say you go, girl!"

"I do love your nut bread," Nancy confessed.

"And how many loaves will you bring?" Misha asked with a doubtful tone.

"One hundred of each!" Dara declared confidently.

"Right, two hundred loaves of bread! Just how do you intend to do that? Get real." Misha was her usual defeatist self.

"Let me worry about that! I can do this!"

And so she did. The next year she went to the White Owl festival by herself. Nancy and Halley were committed to other obligations; Nancy to her new boyfriend, and Halley to her job at Macy's. Misha, no longer part of the group, wasn't invited.

Undeterred, Dara spent three days nearly around the clock in full zucchini-banana production. Once she fell asleep on the tiny floor of her apartment kitchen waiting for the next batch to bake.

In a moment of total commitment, Dara spent nearly all of her small savings on the six-foot banner that announced 'Dara's Delights – Homemade Marvels – By the Slice or Loaf!' At the last minute, she added ... 'and the Butter's Free!'

She draped the banner across her sofa and would stand with a silly grin on her face, just admiring her name in bright red print.

The morning of the big day she was up at four a.m. The banana nut bread was wrapped in commercial plastic wrap and tied with yellow ribbon. The zucchini bread was tied with bright green. She bought two five-pound tubs of whipped butter, a commercial metal frosting knife, and a thousand six-inch paper plates. If she forgot anything, she thought, she would just make do. As she pulled into the dawn-lit highway, she began to sing at the top of her voice I've Got Confidence, from her favorite movie, The Sound of Music.

As Dara pulled into White Owl an hour later than planned, the streets were teeming with recent arrivals. The traffic came to an abrupt stop right in front of The Clothes Closet. The intersection was the divider for traffic proceeding to the music venues, and the vendor step-up and parking. Though still a couple blocks away, tickets were being checked, and vendor ID badges checked.

Dara took in her surroundings and her excitement grew.

"We're almost there!" she said to no one.

The old building on her left was in rough shape. The sign had fallen down or was removed years before. Multiple layers, and just as many colors, of paint, peeled and flaked, revealing the building's long history.

Dara sighed and said, "Poor old girl, doesn't anybody love you anymore?"

At that moment a cloud passed in front of the sun that sent a slender beam of light exposing the metallic sheen of the words Moon Café. The Ming's old gold paint, for just a brief moment, gleamed like new.

"Nice!" Dara squealed as the cloud rolled by and the traffic moved forward. "Was that for me?"

The Festival didn't officially open until in the morning, but people came early to secure their camping spots and seats in the meadow or amphitheater. At the end of Main Street, Dara flashed her vendor badge with a wide smile and was waved through. A tall gray-haired man with a clipboard and orange vest approached Dara's car window.

"Good afternoon, pretty lady."

"Good afternoon to you, handsome sir!" Dara returned.

"Badge number?"

"1889, Dara Landry."

"Alright, you will be in booth # 26. Nice spot."

"Really?"

"Yep, right at the intersection. Traffic from both streets intermingle. Everybody is going to see your...?"

"Banana Nut Bread and Chocolate Zucchini Bread!" Dara replied. "Come by. The first piece is on me."

"I'll be sure and do that. I'm Carl."

"I'm Dara," she said, sticking her hand through the car window."

"You're up ahead on the right. Numbers on the front of the table. When you finish unloading, you can park in the bank lot behind your booth."

"Thank you, Carl."

Just as she was told, her booth was right on the corner. Dara pulled up and got out and stood for a moment looking at the imposing eight feet of white plastic table in front of her.

"How am I going to fill that?"

"It's smaller than it looks." A woman's voice came from behind Dara.

"Oh, hi," Dara said, turning. "I thought I was by myself."

"I talk to myself too. The shrink says, 'it's okay so long as I don't answer.'" The woman extended her hand, "I'm Cathy Walker, you already met by better half."

"Carl?"

"Yep, twenty-six years. So what are you selling?"

"Chocolate zucchini and banana nut bread."

"Oh, Rhonda won't like that. Good for you!"

"Who's Rhonda?"

"Preacher's wife. Thinks her banana nut bread is God's gift to the world." Cathy wrinkled her nose. "Too dry for my taste."

"You'll have to come by and try mine. See how it compares." Dara smiled confidently.

"Will do. If you need help with anything let me know. My son Mitch is around here somewhere. He's the fix-it guy. Do you need electricity?"

"No, but I might need some help hanging my banner," Dara said, looking up at the two poles on the ends of the booth.

"Then he's your guy. I'll send him over."

The table was way too big for Dara's needs. She tried to figure out how to display her breads, but even if she put out every loaf, the table would swallow them. The loaves were carefully packed in large plastic tubs. Each layer was supported by sixteen-ounce cups in the corners and one in the middle. The tubs allowed for forty loaves each. The five tubs filled the trunk and back seat of the car. Her banner and sleeping bag rode beside her along with the ice chest full of butter.

First order of the day was to get the banner up. Dara plopped the plastic roll onto the table and realized that her sign was six feet long, not eight. This is just not what I figured on, she thought. For the first time, her confidence was beginning to show signs of cracking. What have I got myself into? She glared down at the banner she took such great delight in the night before with disgust.

"Are you the one that needs some help?" Off to Dara's left approached a tall, auburn-haired man in an Eagles t-shirt.

"Yeah, I'm feeling a bit overwhelmed at the moment."

"What seems to be the problem?" he frowned.

"I got a six-foot banner and an eight-foot table. If I put everything out I brought, it will look like I'm half sold out, or at worst, have nothing to offer."

"Are you always such a ray of sunshine?"

"What's that supposed to mean?" Dara snapped.

"Nothin', you're just kind of a Debbie Downer. I bet you'd be pretty if you smiled."

"Well, Studly, I'm just not in the mood for your Alpha Male come on."

"Okay," he said softly, embarrassed by his fumble. "What if you just use one table? I'll put one behind you and you can keep part of your inventory there. These poles," he said, grabbing on, "are on stands and I can roll them wherever. What do you think?"

"That would be perfect!" Dara's confidence was on the mend.

Her handsome helper went to work separating the tables. Dara went to the car, suddenly in a panic. Did she forget her table signs? Oh, you've got to be kidding, she scolded herself. She moved her sleeping bag and ice chest, nothing. She crawled into the back seat and looked under the front seats, nothing. After she removed the tubs from the trunk, she scoured the trunk for any of her homemade signs complete with cut out daisies, descriptions, and prices. They were nowhere to be found.

"Is there a stationary store or school supply store in town?"

"Yeah, Olson's just up the block."

"Wonderful!" Dara said, showing her relief.

"They're closed though. Most of the merchants took this weekend off because you guys fill up the street. Most of the stores along here are not what festival-goers are after anyway." There was a slight groan as he pulled over one of the poles. "Whatcha need?"

"Oh, I left my table signs at home."

"That sucks."

"And he's articulate. Never mind."

Within a few minutes, the banner was up and the tables rearranged. "How's that?" he asked.

"Much better. Thank you." Dara paused for a long moment looking at her helper. "I'm sorry if I was a bit nasty with you."

"A bit?" There was a pleasing quality to Dara's helper as he shyly teased.

"Okay, a lot. I apologize. I'm Dara."

"Mitch Walker."

"Yeah, your mom said."

"Alright, I have extension cords to run and panic attacks to talk down. Good luck tomorrow. If you need anything else, my folks are always wandering around somewhere."

"Thank you, Mitch," Dara said coyly. "Sorry again about the..."

"No problem. See you later."

"Come back for some..." Dara spoke to Mitch's back as he turned and made his way up the street. He either didn't hear her or didn't care.

Bright and early the next morning, long before the other vendors, Dara was lugging her tubs from the bank parking lot and to her table. She slept in the back seat of her car and seemed to wake up every time the volunteer night watchman came through shining his flashlight in all the car and truck windows. Still, she was wide awake and excited for the first sale of the day. That sale turned out to be Carl.

"Good morning, I'm here to collect my free slice!" Carl held up a large coffee mug. "Think it'll go good with this?"

"Perfect!" Dara said cheerfully. "Banana nut or chocolate zucchini?"

"Never had chocolate zucchini. Let's go with that!"

"Coming right up!" Dara turned and popped the lid off the tube tagged with a Z. "There you are!" she exclaimed. Sitting on the top of the loaves of zucchini bread were her table signs.

"What'd you find?" Carl queried.

"The perfect start of my day, I found my missing table signs!"

"You made quite an impression on my son Mitch," Carl said, slyly.

"Yeah, Debbie Downer is a hit at every party."

"He called you that?"

"I didn't blame him, I was kind of snarky."

"We have a tough time getting him to even talk to girls, let alone insult them. You are more than just a pretty face."

Dara could feel her face redden as she cut a thick slice of the bread. "Butter?"

"Don't tell my wife." Carl smiled.

Dara handed the piece of zucchini bread to Carl. He looked at it closely.

"This has got real, like garden-grown, green, tubular zucchini in it?"

"The grocery store variety, but, yeah. What do you think?" Dara watched as Carl took a bite and chewed.

"A lot better than the zucchini crap Cathy makes with tomatoes and garlic."

"I'll take that as a compliment," Dara said, hopefully.

"For sure it is! This is great. The gates are about to open. I'll catch you later." Carl turned to walk away. He turned back and said, "Good luck today. And if you see Mitch, be nice!" He laughed and continued down the street.

She didn't see Mitch that day. What she did see were hundreds of people coming by her table and buying her baked goods, fifty cents a slice or three dollars a loaf. The gates opened at eight and by two o'clock there was not a loaf of her breads left. Not knowing quite what to do, Dara sat for nearly a half-hour on the table, feet gently kicking back and forth, and seven hundred and sixty-five dollars in her apron.

She was preparing to leave when a large woman with a bright green checkered apron approached the table.

"I came to try some of your banana nut bread I've been hearing so much about."

"I'm sorry, I'm all sold out," Dara replied.

"Well, sweetie, this is a big event. Not like a high school bake sale. You need more than a few loaves to get through the weekend."

"I brought two hundred loaves. I didn't know how many to bring, really. Next year I'll plan for more."

"How many?" The woman asked.

"Two hundred, a hundred banana nut and a hundred chocolate zucchini. I was afraid I'd be eating it for months if it didn't sell." Dara laughed. "Do you have a booth too?"

"Yes," the woman said curtly.

"I'm Dara."

"Rhonda."

"Oh, the pastor's wife! Nice to meet you. Sales going good?"

Rhonda whirled around and said, "Maybe they will be now." And off she went down the street.

It took a bit of doing, but Dara was able to pull over the poles and untie her banner. She hummed I've Got Confidence as she carefully rolled up the banner. "Dara's Delights, indeed!" she said, as she put the banner under her arm, picked up the stack of empty tubs, and headed for her car.

As she rounded the corner of the bank, a voice called out, "Where you goin'?" It was Cathy, walking quickly towards her.

"Oh, hello! All sold out! What a great day!"

"Will you be back next year?"

"For sure! Put me on the list. Want me to pay now?"

"No, no we'll send you the application next spring. I'm so happy you did well. I saw Rhonda stomping off from your booth." Cathy laughed. "She hasn't sold diddly. I love it!"

"Oh, come on," Dara said, frowning.

"No, she's madder than a boiled owl. She's been just sitting down there. Even the locals are talking about your stuff. Carl was nuts about your chocolate zucchini bread. I meant to get over and get a loaf."

"Next year I'll bring you a loaf. I just love this town!"

"It seems to have taken a shine to you, too! Especially, Mitch. What did you say to the kid? He's like a different person."

"Nothing, really, honest, nothing. He was so sweet. I was kind of snotty to him. Please tell him how sorry I am, I was out of line."

"No problem. Have you got somebody? Boyfriend, or...? Oh, gee, that's tacky. Forget I asked. It's a mother thing."

"Nope, free as a bird and open to possibilities." Dara smiled, knowing she wouldn't be back for a year. Anything could happen in a year.

"Here, let me give you a hand." Cathy took the tubs and walked Dara to her car.

On the way out of town, she smiled as she passed the Moon Café. "See ya later!"

Dara was a vendor for the next two years. Mitch was waiting for her the next year and they got along much better. She brought six hundred loaves, two hundred each of the banana nut and chocolate zucchini, and two hundred of a new addition, chocolate chip banana. By noon the second day, all six hundred were sold.

To celebrate, she accepted an invitation to dinner with Mitch. Dara ended up staying at Cathy and Carl's an extra day. Mitch showed her the town, told of his plans to become a fireman and how, in the winter, he drove the snowplow. Dara found the bashful, small-town hunk quite charming, and when she left they exchanged numbers and promised to stay in touch. In a moment of abandon, Dara gave Mitch a big kiss on the cheek.

In the months that followed, they chatted, emailed, and texted each other often. In December she came the day after Christmas and rode shotgun in the snowplow, and gave Mitch their first real kiss. As much as Dara hated to admit it, she was falling for Mitch, his family, and the little town.

Dara came three times to visit White Owl that year. Work kept her from visiting more. On Valentine's Day, she received a dozen roses and a simple note from Mitch that said. "You're the one!"

Dara confided in Halley at lunch one day that she was in love with her firefighter boyfriend. "I think we just might end up married! Can you believe it? He hasn't asked or anything, but come spring, don't be surprised."

Dara married Mitch in June of that year. Rhonda's husband officiated and the whole town seemed to turn out. Halley was maid of honor, Nancy was her bridesmaid. Mitch asked his lifelong friend, Ryan, to be his best man, and a very handsome fellow fireman was his groomsman.

Halley and the groomsman dated on and off for a few months but the distance was too big an issue.

Dara loved her new in-laws. Her parents divorced when she was little and she never heard from her father again. During Dara's third year of high school, her mother remarried. Their relationship was permanently damaged. She hadn't spoken to her mother in several years and received no RSVP for her wedding invitation.

The newlyweds settled into a two-bedroom A-Frame just outside of town. Dara became a perfect housewife and worked part-time at Olson's Stationery.

Shortly after their third anniversary, Mitch went with a group from Washington to fight California forest fires. The money was really good, and they planned to put the extra away to start a family the following year.

Dara's Delights made their sixth appearance at the Music Festival street fair. As always, her baked goods were a huge hit. The line expanded to six items. She arranged through a friend to use the kitchen at the elementary school to produce her biggest inventory ever. She recruited Halley to help her work the booth, now expanded to the full eight feet.

Dara was loved by the town's people, and Carl and Cathy insisted she stay a couple of nights a week while Mitch was away. She began to think seriously about having a baby. Mitch made good money, and they were looking into buying a bigger house. She was happier than at any time in her life.

Dara smiled and waved as she saw her mother and father-in-law coming up the street toward her booth. She was giving a customer their change when the pair stepped up to the booth.

Dara's stomach jerked hard when she looked up into Cathy's red-eyed, tear-stained face. She looked quickly to Carl. He was pale and seemed to be struggling to breathe.

"What's wrong?" Dara asked.

"It is Mitch, sweetie. He's been killed," Carl said.

Dara heard nothing after that. She vaguely remembered Halley taking her in her arms, feeling her hot cheek, and the sound of her sobbing.

There were no remains to be returned to White Owl. A flag-covered casket sat at the front of the church where they took their vows. Mitch's White Owl Fire Department helmet sat atop the casket, but Dara knew the wooden box was empty. She refused to go to Carl and Cathy's after the funeral. She didn't want to hear anyone say how sorry they were, what a great guy Mitch was, or if there was anything they could do, just ask. She went home alone. Dara laid in their bed and listened to Mitch's favorite Eagles album over and over.

In the days to come, she considered going back to Portland, but the idea was soon dismissed, White Owl was now her home.

About the Author

Micheal Maxwell has traveled the globe on the lookout for strange sights, sounds, and people. His adventures have taken him from the Jungles of Ecuador and the Philippines to the top of the Eiffel Tower and the Golden Gate Bridge, and from the cave dwellings of Native Americans to The Kehlsteinhaus, Hitler's Eagles Nest! He's always looking for a story to tell and interesting people to meet.

Micheal Maxwell was taught the beauty and majesty of the English language by Bob Dylan, Robertson Davies, Charles Dickens, and Leonard Cohen.

Mr. Maxwell has dined with politicians, rock stars and beggars. He has rubbed shoulders with priests and murderers, surgeons and drug dealers, each one giving him a part of themselves that will live again in the pages of his books.

Micheal Maxwell has found a niche in the mystery, suspense, genre with The Cole Sage Series that gives readers an everyman hero, short on vices, long on compassion, and a sense of fair play, and the willingness to risk everything to right wrongs. The Cole Sage Series departs from the usual, heavily sexual, profanity-laced norm and gives readers character-driven stories, with twists, turns, and page-turning plot lines.

Micheal Maxwell writes from a life of love, music, film, and literature. Along with his lovely wife and travel partner, Janet, divide their time between a small town in the Sierra Nevada Mountains of California, and their lake home in Washington State.

Made in the USA
Columbia, SC
27 April 2021